PRAISE FOR THE LEGEND OF FORENIA: THE TWILIGHT KINGDOM

"Outstanding! Author T.J. Martinell has done it again! This time, it's a pulp fantasy that is packed with action, flowing dialogue, and a story worthy of the swords-and-sorcery classics. Give us more, please!" — Vincent J. LaRosa, *Masculine Geek*

"A wonderfully imaginative tale of a young man's search for his place in the world. I enjoyed it immensely." — K.H. Mezek, author of *Luminaria*

"When Jed Hayes inadvertently travels through a portal in the snow and finds himself in another world, he becomes part of a legendary quest as he joins up with Kara, the last remaining scribe of the Forenian language. Along with her loyal guardian, Telman, Jed and Kara attempt to form a resistance against General Grancaliga, a man whose ambitions drive him to want to become a god. Following the triad as they battle impossible odds in their flight from danger and attempt to pursue the threads of an ancient legend is a gripping adventure. It's well worth the read." — Leslie D. Soule, author of *Fallenwood* and *My Mentor, Death*

ALSO BY T.J. MARTINELL

THE LEGEND OF FORENIA

OF

THE TWILIGHT KINGDOM

T.J. Martinell

Sheridan, WY
Terror House Press
2021

ISBN 978-1-951897-61-1

EDITOR

Matt Forney (mattforney.com)

LAYOUT AND COVER DESIGN

Matt Lawrence (mattlawrence.net)

Excerpts of this book were published, in somewhat different form, by *Terror House Magazine*. The author would like to thank *Terror House* for their support.

TERROR HOUSE PRESS, LLC

terrorhousepress.com

TABLE OF CONTENTS

PROLOGUE

Young Kara wept quietly as she gazed out the castle tower window at the triumphant hordes of General Grancaliga's army marching through the capital city of Merce Haelle far below. Though they seemed small and harmless from her lofty position situated within the upper level of the ancient mountainside fortress, like a pestilence, the soldiers quickly swarmed through the streets and arrived at the main castle gate in the lower levels.

Tears slowly trickled down the 16-year-old's pale cheeks as the mighty gate and portcullis rose in anticipation of the advance column approaching the bridge spanning the deep moat. As they drew near, the guards on the watchtowers dropped their weapons and, with bowed heads, collected near the gate.

Kara's amber eyes glowed as she left the window and stood in the center of her small room, the harsh cold wind blowing her long bluish white hair over her headscarf. Every time she seemed to regain her composure, another victorious roar from the city overwhelmed her.

In her hands, she clutched a bundle of manuscripts like a newborn infant, her chin lowered as she wiped away any tears before they fell on the fragile parchment. Carefully, she tucked the manuscripts inside her ice blue cloak, reaching for a small bag near her bed.

"How could it have come to this?" she whispered as she clasped her hands together in prayer. Her voice was faint as she raised her eyes to the ceiling.

The door abruptly opened as Telman entered. A rugged man in his mid-thirties, he wore a similar ice blue cloak over his leather armor. The end of his longsword's scabbard stuck out from beneath the edge of his cloak. He had a somber but determined look on his face. In the hallway behind him were several armed men. Their faces were battered and bloodied, their equipment worn and dirty.

"These are the only Varexians left," Telman said to Kara. "They've secured some horses for us. The old deer path leading outside the city is still open. But we must leave now."

She was silent for a moment. "They just gave it up…"

"Everyone has given up…except you."

"And you?"

Telman offered a wearied smile. "You and I don't have that right."

Kara nodded as she threw her cloak hood over her head. She joined Telman at the door. She looked back into the room at the desk in the corner.

"Oh, Telman, I do hope we come back here someday," she said.

"I as well…if Grancaliga doesn't burn it."

Taking her hand, he pulled her into the corridor, closed the door, and joined the Varexians waiting for them in the corridor.

Minutes later, the door flew back as soldiers stormed into the room, their faces concealed by their thick helmets. Their grey tunics blended flawlessly with their heavy chainmail. With loosened grips, they held their short swords down at their sides. They surveyed the room for a moment, then called out into the corridor.

More soldiers arrived. Then they all stood erect as Grancaliga stooped under the doorway and entered the room. In his early forties, he was at least a head taller than the others. His white hair was cropped, his ascetic face clean and shaved. Like his soldiers, he wore a grey tunic clung tightly to his lean frame by a thick leather belt. His great sword was sheathed in a large scabbard slung over his back.

For a while, he was quiet. His presence left the soldiers in a tense state. Then he turned to one of his colonels standing behind him and spoke. His voice was like a bear's growl, but smooth and subtle.

"Whose private chambers is this?" he asked.

"Kara, daughter of Reginald. She's one of the few castle residents still unaccounted for."

"Who else is missing?"

"Telman."

Grancaliga chuckled softly. "I break the Varexian Army in a single day, the Elder Council votes to surrender, and now all Forenia is in my hands. Yet he *still* won't quit."

A messenger appeared and whispered in the colonel's ear. Puzzled, he gestured for the man to stay as he hesitantly drew near to Grancaliga. "Sir, apparently the archive is empty; the religious and historical manuscripts are gone. One of our curriers also saw a small band of men on horse headed west from the castle."

Grancaliga's eyes narrowed on the desk. Approaching it with a sense of unfamiliarity, he opened one of the drawers. An unsettled expression fell across his face as he took out pieces of blank parchment, a quill pen, and an inkwell. He placed them on the desk before turning to the colonel.

"Have a small detachment of your best men ready to leave within the hour," he said.

"What is happening?"

A brief exchange of looks with his general, and the colonel ordered the soldiers out of the room. He then approached Grancaliga by the desk. "Are we pursuing Telman? He's no threat at this point."

"The girl is."

"How?"

He pointed at the items on the desk. "She can read our language...*and* write. Who else would have taken the religious texts except her? She is only person who can actually understand them."

The words left the colonel speechless for moment as he studied the desk. "Where do you think she is headed?"

Grancaliga frowned. "Have you truly forgotten the legend?"

The colonel seemed perplexed at first, then his eyes widened. "Sir, forgive my boldness, but Impora is a beloved Forenian myth, nothing more."

"Clearly, she believes otherwise. Besides, we know the king's crown sealed within the top of this mountain *is* real. If she can read the text, she will know how to open the door, and she'll know the Divinity Prayer."

He paused, his gauntlet-clad hand forming a powerful fist. "As long as the crown exists, there will still be those with hope that a king will wear it once again. My rule must be absolute, or it is nothing at all."

He loomed over the colonel with his imposing stature. While both shared the same amber eyes, Grancaliga's gaze radiated a willpower so great it made the man tremble. "We must recover the girl at all costs…and *alive.*"

The colonel bowed. "I will assemble the men at once and instruct them accordingly!"

He departed, leaving Grancaliga alone in the room. He stared at the desk, then moved over to the window overlooking Merce Haelle. The entire capital was alit with torches as the soldiers paraded through the streets singing war songs in honor of their commander.

Smiling to himself, Grancaliga went back to the desk and picked up the items, holding the quill pen close to his face. "Merce Haelle will be the crown jewel of my kingdom. Yet it's nothing compared to what now I've found."

Placing the pen on the desk, he looked out and up high at the candlestick-like peaks of the Perelor Mountains scarcely visible in the great distance. "I was content to merely be supreme guardian. Now, I will become a god."

CHAPTER 1

Jed Hayes wondered how there could be snow in the middle of summer as he glanced at the small pile of white beside the tree behind him. Sitting on a park bench near the local baseball field, he turned and stared at the snow before blinking rapidly to see if he was seeing things. His thoughts of bewilderment were blurred by the banter from nearby children playing tag on the large grass field.

A man appeared on the sidewalk. Jed looked up eagerly, only to back down when he realized it wasn't his father. To someone who didn't know, the 17-year-old acted like he was expecting a Hollywood celebrity to arrive instead of "Lieutenant Colonel Hayes," back after completing the final active duty assignment of his career. Any minute now, he was supposed to arrive, the first time the two had seen one another in months.

Jed was like his father, possessing a medium height and build that had aided every man in the Hayes family for 200 years rucking across America, Europe and everywhere else in an Army uniform. His unusual maturity, frequently noted by friends and family, contrasted with youthful, boyish features unblurred by hardship or experience. It was that disconnect or something else about him that had recently convinced his father he wasn't ready for Junior Army ROTC, much to his son's dismay. Jed hoped to change his father's mind while they played catch and caught up on life, having spent the last hour thinking of how to bring it up in a strategical manner.

Leaning back on the bench as he whittled on a piece of wood with his Boy Scout pocketknife, he caught sight of a cute girl his age sitting on the grass with a book in hand. When their eyes locked for a moment, he suddenly grew shy and looked back at the pile of snow.

Unable to contain his curiosity, he got up from the park bench and placed his hand on the snow. The wet, cold feeling on his fingertips felt real enough. He pushed his fingers down further.

An eerie sensation ran through his hand and up his arm. He tried to pull his hand out, but a magnetic-like force pulled him closer to the snow until his head was went in. On the other side, the snow was gone. He found himself in a freefall amid a kaleidoscope-like vortex of multicolored rays as bright as the northern lights. His senses dazed by a loud, distant noise like that of a crashing wave, he was unable to think or even fear what was happening.

Within the vortex, time did not seem to exist. It felt like a thousand years as much a mere instant. The experience reminded him of the Gravitron ride at the local county fair, except now he didn't have that sick feeling his gut making him want to vomit.

Without warning, he landed on soft ground. After a numb moment, he began shivering as the wet, cold sensation of snow returned to his fingertips. Slowly opening his eyes, he struggled to make out his environment. His vision improved until he could make out the scenery.

Around him was a vast mountain range unlike anything he had seen before; pale blue-shaded peaks were like jagged columns, shrouded in soft snow that continued to fall gently and silently. The peaks rose from the narrow ridgelines and into the thick, misty clouds.

Glancing down at his feet, he looked at his T-shirt and shorts. Taking long, deep breaths, he fought back the anxiety swelling inside as he trudged through the snowdrifts. An aching pain soon developed in his feet as he lost sensation in his toes. Spotting an arched curve along the mountainside, he walked toward it and found a cave.

Throwing himself inside it, he took off his soaked shoes and socks and placed them aside. He hastily recalled his wilderness survival training. He already found shelter, but he needed to find a way to get dry and locate food. He held his feet in his hands to warm them properly as he searched the cave. There was nothing except strange-looking rocks. He would have to go elsewhere once he got his feet dry. But then he would have to find a way to protect them.

He glanced out the cave. Straining his eyes, he thought he saw figures out along the ridgeline.

Blinking rapidly, he looked again.

The faintly visible figures continued to move.

Watching them in silence, his gaze followed their movements as they ascended the ridgeline across from his cave. He took another long breath and exhaled.

He had to risk it. He had no idea where he was or how he had even gotten there. But it seemed certain that no food would be found outside. Even if he did, his clothes could not keep him alive through the night.

Bracing himself for the cold once more, he dashed outside. Hurrying as best he could along the ridgeline, he called out to the figures now headed in the opposite direction. The wind blasting between the peaks overtook his calls. Growing weary from pushing through the snow, he grew anxious as he cried out louder.

He pushed all his strength into his legs; thanks to his physical training regimen, he was able to close the distance. By then, he could make out the people better. Their long blue coats seemed dyed in the same light reflecting off the peaks.

He called a final time, and again, no one heard him. Summoning the last ounce of energy within him, he broke into a sprint and reached the last person in the group. Gasping for breath and his lungs charred from the frigid air, he lunged out and grabbed their shoulder.

Before he could even touch them, the figure spun around and threw him on the ground, a sword already drawn. Disoriented, Jed was too exhausted to protest as the figure placed the blade's tip against his throat, his face concealed by the hood placed far down over his forehead.

"Stop," a female voice called.

Cautiously, the figure brought back the blade and sheathed it. A small person knelt beside Jed and pulled back their hood.

His eyes were wide and large as he looked at a girl. She seemed human and had a gentle expression, but her complexion and hair were as white as a corpse.

"What are you?" she said.

Jed tried to speak, but drifted off into unconsciousness. As he did, he could hear the girl pleading with her companions while she brought his head up from the snow and placed it in her lap.

***

Jed woke to the soft warmth of a small fire in front of him. A blanket had been placed beneath him, a pack serving as a pillow. The girl was sitting near him concernedly. The other figures stood above her. Like her, their humanoid faces and hair were a deathly white, and they looked at him with the same amber eyes.

He kept silent.

The girl offered him a drink from a canteen. "Feeling better?"

Jed nodded as he took small sips. Despite their different appearances, she seemed friendly enough. She waited for him to talk until it was evident she would have to initiate.

"I'm Kara. What is your name?"

"Jed."

One of the men approached the girl and spoke over her shoulder. "We have to go." He then spoke to Jed suspiciously. "Know how to fight?"

Jed tried not to smile as he nodded. It was good for them to know he was useful, but he still did not have the slightest clue what was going on. He preferred to say as little as required.

Intrigued, the man reached into a large pack and handed Jed a pair of trousers and the same tunic they all wore underneath their cloaks. Jed hastily put them on, then a pair of hefty knee-high boots the man gave him. He was amazed at how light they felt, but were as warm as a down jacket.

With reluctance, the man then handed him a short sword. "I'm Telman. I can tell you don't know where you are or how you got here, but I don't have time to say anything else. I just know you're not an enemy, and that's enough. Do as you're told, and be prepared to fight if it comes to that. Stay back with Kara here and keep her safe. Do you understand?"

Jed gestured affirmatively.

The band quickly gathered their things, heaped a pile of snow on the fire, then continued trudging across the ridgeline. Telman took point while the other four men followed shortly behind him. Kara and Jed remained back, but not too far away. For a while, they remained silent as they walked. Jed wanted to learn more, to find out where he was. Yet, he felt guarded about revealing anything.

Kara watched him glancing up at the pike-like peaks around them. "The Perelor Mountains. Are they not beautiful? I've never seen them before, except the illustrations. I always wondered if they were truly this tall."

Eventually, they came to a point where the ridge became so narrow that they had to walk with one foot in front of the other. On both sides was nothing but a steep drop into a murky abyss. Retrieving a rope from his gear, Telman walked carefully across the section of the ridge, then tied the rope to a rock and tossed it across to the others. One of them then tied the other end around another rock. Gripping it tight, they each took slow steps as they crossed.

When it came for Kara's turn, she grasped the rope and began moving forward. Her foot slipped, causing her knees to buckle. As she regained her composure, a bundle in her cloak fell out. Frantic, she grabbed it with an outstretched hand. Unable to keep her grip on the rope, she began to slide off the ridge.

Anticipating her fall, Jed leapt over to her and grabbed her hand. Pulling her up, he helped her regain her hold on the rope. On the other side, Telman was aghast. However, he waited until she was safely across before he chastised her. "You cannot be that reckless."

"I was going to lose the manuscripts."

"There's no point if you're dead."

He then had Jed cut the rope loose behind him and then walk it across the ridgeline.

"I'm impressed," he whispered in Jed's ear, placing a firm hand on his shoulder. The gesture reminded Jed of his youngest uncle, Vern. He had always been there to care for him and his mother when his father was away. Content to remain a captain, the Army had moved him and his family to the other side of the country just the year prior.

The group continued onward between two peaks. The wind was so strong it felt as though it might lift Jed up from the ground. Unable to fight it, they eventually took shelter behind a large slab. Telman and the other men remained huddled together and talked amongst themselves. Kara sat beside Jed and listened to the wind.

"Thank you for saving me just now," she said as she opened her cloak and showed him the bundle now firmly tied to her belt. "I had to save these. You don't know how important they are."

Jed raised his eyebrow curiously as he gestured at them.

"They're our religious texts," she said. She was about to say more, but stopped herself. "That's right, you don't know where you are. This is Forenia. How did you come here?"

"I'm trying to figure out that myself."

Self-conscious of how she gawked at him, she laughed. "I'm sorry for staring, but I've never seen anyone who looks like you before. Forenians are the only people here. There might be in other places, but we've never been able to venture that far out."

Telman called to them. "The wind is dying down. We'll give it another minute, then we go."

Kara buttoned up her cloak. As they walked again, she spoke to Jed. "It's not that we can't travel. We have old maps. But nobody wants to. There's only one reason for someone to come here."

Jed was eager to hear more, but Telman interrupted. "We must go faster, or they're going to catch up."

"Who?" Kara asked.

Telman appeared incredulous. "Do you really think he hasn't been tracking us the moment we left the castle?"

She tried hard to hide her apprehension as she brushed her gloved hand against the manuscripts inside her cloak. Her amber eyes looked down before she touched Jed's arm. "Wherever you're from or how you got here, you're certainly come to Forenia at a strange time."

✦✦✦

Grancaliga stood atop his steed at full height as he surveyed the steep pass ahead leading into the Perelor Mountains high above. The scores of soldiers behind him waited on their horses in perfectly formed lines. Their tall banners flapped furiously in the bitter wind as it swept down from the mountainside as though one of his cavalry units in a charge.

Unmoved by the chill on his exposed face, Grancaliga turned to his colonels seated on their horses beside him. "Have the men dismount. Tell the men-at-arms accompanying us to lead the horses back to our nearest outpost and await our return. They are also to investigate the local hamlets. If anyone gave them so much as a morsel of bread, burn everything to the ground."

"How far ahead are they?" they asked.

With an open hand, he cast a spell from his fingertips that fell over the snow, revealing footprints running up the pass.

"Not far," he said. "We are less than a day's journey behind."

"They'll be able to travel faster and lighter."

Grancaliga grinned as he dismounted his horse. "Our men have marched harder than this before for two days and fought a battle afterwards. We will catch up and overtake them."

Inspired by their commander's total confidence, the colonels returned to their ranks and had the soldiers leave their horses. Now afoot, they formed a large single column behind Grancaliga and approached the pass.

"Is it wise for you to travel in the front?" a colonel said. "There could be an ambush. They might be awaiting our arrival."

"No. If there is an ambush, I will be the one to set it."

CHAPTER 2

Jed rapidly drew his sword as he turned in the direction of a wolf howl from somewhere beyond the vast ridgeline. Gripping the handle with one hand, he instinctively grabbed Kara and placed her behind him. The unearthly exclamations poured over the slopes as they ascended the organ pipes-like peaks.

"What are those?" he asked.

Kara placed a reassuring hand on his arm. "Mountain spirits singing hymns to the gods."

Not ready to believe her, Jed waited until no creature appeared before sheathing his blade and resuming their hike upward to join Telman and the others.

Her explanation failed to soothe his nerves, still recovering from the time he and Vern had encountered a pack of wolves on a hunting trip. Each time another wail appeared, his hand automatically touched the hilt and remained there until he was satisfied.

Noticing the pair had fallen back, Telman turned around and waited for them with a concerned demeanor. "What happened?"

"He mistook the mountain spirits for a beast or something," Kara said. "It's certainly what I would have thought if I hadn't read the manuscripts."

Telman listened to the faint melodious voices before shaking his head. "I was wondering what they were, too. Even so, we should stay on our guard. *They* might be harmless…there could be other dangerous things."

"There are no creatures of any kind in these mountains except for the spirits," Kara insisted. "They are no threat if we do not desecrate the mountains."

"How can you be so sure?"

"The manuscripts."

"Are you sure we can trust them?" a Varexian said.

Kara was bewildered. "How could we not?"

"How many years has it been since they were written? At least a thousand, right?"

Her chin rose worriedly. "Would Forena have allowed such an error?"

"Things could have changed in that time."

"The texts have not."

The Varexian pointed at Jed. "Then what is *he* doing in the mountains?"

Everyone looked at Jed, but he refused to take a side by answering. It wasn't his quarrel.

"I imagine you don't live here, right?" Telman said.

Jed nodded.

"Then where did he come from?" the Varexian said.

"I don't know," Telman said before Jed could answer. "I just know he's not one of Grancaliga's spies or assassins."

He then addressed Kara, giving Jed a subtle, reassuring grin. "Speaking of which, I think it's time to consult that map of yours once again." He motioned to the Varexians. "Let's keep following this path until we confirm we're on the right route. I'd rather lead Grancaliga the wrong way than stand here and wait for him to show up."

Pressing hard up as the rising ridgeline, Kara walked closely alongside Telman as she reached into her cloak. Jed took the rear, still maintaining a vigilant watch of the voices. He then joined the two as Kara brought out a faded parchment with a map drawn on it. Telman held a part of his cloak over her head to keep it dry. Whatever language it was, the words were too small for Jed to see through the snowfall.

Her studious eyes roaming across the map, Kara's fingers delicately touched the parchment's surface as they followed a line drawn through a collection of illustrated mountain peaks.

Inhaling hard, she put the map away and spoke in a hushed voice to Telman. Hesitant at first, he then called to the Varexians again. "We turn north here."

The Varexians appeared incredulous. The one who had spoken before broke from the group and confronted Telman. "There's no way through."

"The map says there will be a passageway somewhere."

"And if not?"

"The map says it's there," Kara said.

The Varexian stared at her. "What *you* say."

"There's no point in arguing. I'm the only person who can read this map…or anything else, for that matter."

The Varexian didn't move. Nor did the other soldiers.

"All our hope is in you," he said to Kara. "Hope that you read that map correctly, hope that you know how to read at all…that you aren't just making this up because you can't accept that there is no hope."

"I believe her," Jed said.

"Why? You don't even know her. You don't even know where you are."

Jed pointed at Telman. "I know he's somebody to be trusted. If he believes her, so do I. So should you."

Readjusting the shield on his back, the soldier nodded to the other Varexians, and they returned to Telman.

"We head north, yes?" the Varexian said.

Kara nodded. "The passageway will be there."

"I hope you're right."

Acting as though the argument hadn't occurred, Telman once more took over leading the group. Kara smiled at Jed as if pleasantly surprised, then selectively stepped into the deep snow prints left in front of them by Telman. They then turned left toward what seemed to be an impregnable wall of ice-clad rock that eventually separated into spike-like peaks and disappeared into the shadowy mist.

Looking back at Jed, Telman waved an invitation to join him at the front. When he did, Telman patted him on the shoulder and spoke in his ear. "Once more, you impress me."

✳✳✳

"Can we stop and eat?" Kara asked. "We haven't had a meal since we left."

"Eat all you want, but we don't stop," Telman called back to her from the front. He then noticed how Jed had perked up at the mention of food. "Get something. We won't eat again until nightfall."

Jed walked back to where Kara took out a small bag tied to her trouser belt. From it, she produced some type of brownish gold bread that, once cracked, seemed to break apart on its own.

"Try some," she said. "It's my recipe."

Jed took a bite. It tasted sweeter than Southern iced tea. Yet the richness didn't overwhelm him.

"It's good, isn't it?" Kara said as she offered more. He ate all she gave, then took a drink from her canteen. The water was equally sweet. Within minutes, he felt as though waking from a sound night's sleep.

"It has magical properties," she said as she saw his eyes widen. "You put a potion in it while you make. Something ordinary Forenians can learn. Tell me, can you read your language?"

Jed nodded.

"It is so fascinating to think of such a place," Kara said, her eyes wandering off. "I'm the only one in the entire kingdom who reads ancient Forenian."

When Jed looked at her with skepticism, she smiled with such pride that a touch of rouge red appeared on her white cheeks. "I come from a scribe family. They were the only people able to read and study our religious and historical texts. When the last king died without an heir, two rivals fought for the throne. One of them sought to kill all the scribes who had sided against them. Only my ancestor survived the purge. He destroyed all his writing material, then used a potion to conceal himself as an ordinary blacksmith. Later, he managed to regain residence inside the royal castle after the Truce of Belead. Since then, we've kept the knowledge a secret within the family and the castle as our home…until today."

She took a final bite of bread and then put the bag away. She glanced at Jed nervously as if trying to hold something back. He didn't press her.

She sighed heavily. "I can't tell the others this, but I have to admit I'm afraid I'll never see home again. I know I shouldn't think about it, but I can't help it. It's the only home I've ever known, I know nothing else will replace it. Please tell me: are you afraid of that, too?"

With his eyes fixed ahead, Jed stirred his head slightly. "I have no idea how I got here. So how can I get back home?"

"I understand," she said. "You're like me. You want to go home, but can't. For now."

She held her small hands together in prayer, listening reverently to the hymns of the mountain spirits. The once-fearsome strains had transformed into delicate chants evoking memories of Jed's church choir. It had a soothing effect on him, and his relaxed hand drifted away from his sword hilt.

"We'll get back home, both of us," Kara said as she ended her prayer. "I promise."

***

The long column of soldiers stretched back across the ridgeline and down the slope as they pushed speedily through the snow. Grancaliga stood off to the side at the midway point where he could be seen by all, accompanied by his standard-bearer. The bright grand flag of the Guardian Army flew steadily as it flapped violently in the wind.

He observed his soldiers with admiration. They had done a forced march since Merce Haelle. Yet their backs were still straight, saluting him as they passed as though in parade formation. They seemed deaf to the apparent voices bellowing from the mountains.

Up ahead, a messenger ran back from the front toward Grancaliga. Spotting him, the colonels joined the general and eagerly waited until the messenger arrived.

"We spotted them headed north," the messenger said.

"Why?" a colonel asked in disbelief. "There's nothing but the mountain wall. They can't possibly climb it."

"We don't need to know," Grancaliga said. "They're headed there. We follow."

He retrieved a map from his satchel and studied it. Unlike Kara's, there were only illustrations on it with lines and ink spots.

"We're beyond any known territory," he said as he put the map away. His amber eyes narrowed cunningly as he turned to the messenger. "How was the ground there?"

"Open. Nearer to the mountain wall the ridge becomes narrow."

"We must get to them before they reach that point. How far before they get there?"

"Half a day's journey."

Grancaliga gazed at the faint glow of Forenia's three suns behind the layered veil of snowfall. He then spoke to the colonels. "Find Arthema."

The colonels left together along the column. They finally stopped and ordered a man out. He saluted them and approached Grancaliga. The tall, lanky man had a thin white longbow slung over his back, along with a long wide quiver stuffed with multicolored arrows. His hair was cut short like Grancaliga's, two arrow-like scars on both cheeks.

"Take your best bowmen and head north, but once you encounter footprints, move northwest. They'll camp for the night somewhere near the rocks for shelter. Wait until the morning, then attack. If any of them somehow survive, they'll head south toward the wall. We will cut them off."

Arthema saluted in high reverence. "It will be done."

Grancaliga's voice was emphatic. "The girl is not to be harmed. I want the manuscripts she has intact as well. Your punishment should you fail... will be to live."

Arthema's eyes wavered for an instant as if a horrid memory returned to him. He saluted again and ran off. With a quick gesture, four fellow bowman broke ranks and followed him closely. Grancaliga watched in delight as they shrank on the horizon, easily outpacing the sentinels placed at the column's front.

"I almost feel cheated," Grancaliga said. "It's too easy."

Telman watched curiously as Jed sat on a rock while running a sharpening stone against his sword. In front of them, the campfire had reduced to glowing embers. All the Varexians slept except for a lookout on a large boulder behind Jed.

Kara slumbered near the fire, her head nestled against her pack. She has gone to bed shortly following their arrival, but not before reciting something from the manuscript she said would protect them. While she did so, Jed had inspected his sword and found the blade's edge somewhat dull. Noting the sharpening stone near Telman's pack, he had taken it and worked the edges.

Now that the fire had dimmed, he could hardly see his hands. He placed the stone near Telman as he held the sword up near the fire, delicately touching the edge with his fingertips.

"Your father's a soldier," Telman said.

Jed looked at him with surprise.

"I can tell," Telman said with a chuckle. "You handle a blade like you've seen one before. Your father a swordsman?"

"He knows knives."

"Is soldering a family thing?"

Jed smiled. "Like Kara and reading."

The remark left Telman even more enthralled. He stood up, drawing his sword. "Preferably you're as skilled in your family profession as hers."

Jed raised his eyebrows, gesturing at Kara and the Varexians. "Won't they hear us?"

"Don't worry, they all took her sleeping potions," Telman said as he walked into a patch of thinly layered snow.

Shrugging, Jed stood and held his blade with his right hand. Telman called to the Varexian so he wouldn't be surprised by the noise.

Jed let Telman make the first move, a swing from up high down to the left. Jed blocked it and used his weight to push Telman to the side. However, Telman maintained his balance with a low stance and swiftly pulled his sword back, then thrust it forward toward Jed's chest. Barely blocking it, Jed again tried to push Telman off balance. Despite his swift movements, the older man held steady. Telman feigned struggle for a moment before he disengaged by pulling his sword away. Then, with a flick of his wrist, he brought the tip to Jed's chest. Just barely missing it in time, the boy lowered his sword in concession. He felt embarrassed; he could easily field dress a deer with his hunting knife, but swordplay felt totally alien to him.

Telman exchanged swords with him, and they continued sparring. Though his blade's length was greater, Jed was still unable to work around the older man's guard. Using his armor-clad elbow, he slid Jed's blade to the side as he held the short sword against his chest.

"You give away your movements," Telman said. "Hold your blade so you can strike quickly."

Jed tried to copy Telman's example, then attacked. This time, he managed to corner Telman against the boulder. When they crossed swords, Telman rotated his blade so Jed's sword locked into his hilt guard. He then spun Jed around and pushed him against the boulder.

Telman seemed pleased. "Your skills could improve. But you're brave. That's far more important."

Leading him by the arm, they returned to their place by the fire. Jed checked his blade and briefly worked the sharpening stone again.

"You don't have the Spark of Forena," Telman said. "Yet you might as well."

"I assume that's a compliment."

"Kara says it's in the manuscripts," Telman said as he pointed at his glowing eyes. "Forena first created our people in the Hercerla Forest. According to the legends, his spirit was so great that it consumed his eyes. They burned fire, as ours do. With that fire, he fashioned the divine sword, Impora."

He looked over at Kara as she slept silently with a peaceful smile. "She and I still believe a king will again rule us. Since the Truce of Belead, Forenia has been divided into small enclaves ever since the king's descendants went into hiding. Several years ago, a military tyrant named Grancaliga raised an army of handpicked men and declared himself Supreme Guardian over all Forenia. His strength and power grew as he conquered each territory, until only Merce Haelle was left to fall."

Telman brought his head down. "His campaign started the same time my father died, and I succeeded him as youngest member ever on the Elder Council. Not much older than you. I had such aspirations. But I found for all the councilmembers' talk of resisting Grancaliga, everything they did was as if his rule was inevitable. My talk of victory was one-sided. I finally realized what was it; they were too scared to fight, but too afraid to give up. It was as if I were the true enemy."

Jed nodded intently. Telman was starting to sound like his father after returning home from work.

Motioning at the Varexian lookout above, Telman lowered his voice. "These men know what happened. Their hope was weak…until they saw the same thing in you I do."

Jed smiled humbly as Telman drew close. "Our position is desperate. Yet I'd rather have a stranger like you with me than ten thousand Forenians. Grancaliga's sword is stained with much innocent blood, but he hopes as dearly as we. His passion inspires not just his men to fight, but myself to resist. My people have done nothing but discourage and betray… save for Kara.

The two men looked at her. She stirred slightly, then was still again. Telman approached her quietly and brought her blanket up over her shoulders.

"For centuries, all we had were the claims of generations long dead that the throne would be reclaimed through Impora," he said. "It's hard to believe in mere stories. But Kara says that's exactly what's written in the manuscripts. We're after the sword. But if Grancaliga gets her first, the throne remains empty forever—if it remains at all."

He uttered a short laugh under his breath. "Perhaps, for once, he'll fail."

"How so?" Jed asked.

"He's finally encountered those who want to win."

***

Arthema gazed out at the obscured encampment in the distance. There was no smoke or silhouettes from campfire flames. He raised his head and took a deep, long breath through his nose, smiling as he opened his eyes.

He grabbed one of his bowmen and brought him close. "We move at dawn. Remember, the girl can't be harmed. Pick your targets well. Don't shoot if you are uncertain."

The bowman nodded and returned to inform the others. Arthema sat atop the heavy boulder, where his gear was laid out neatly. He picked up his bow, covered with scores of short notches. With a knife in hand, he toyed with preemptively carving out more before placing it down.

He chuckled. "Telman's head will make a better trophy."

CHAPTER 3

Jed woke in darkness to the hint of bent sunrays on the obscured horizon. The campfire smoldered in front of him, wisps of smoke seeping from the ashes. The Varexian lookout stood noiselessly on the rock above him.

Kara still slept soundly across from him, as if she hadn't moved since he had gone to bed. Sticking just out of her blanket were the bundled manuscripts tucked closely against her chest and covered by her long hair.

Jed threw off his blanket and approached the campfire to warm his hands as he slipped leather gauntlets on them. Sitting beside Telman, he noted his large triangular-curved shield beside him, similar to the one in his father's study bearing the Hayes Family coat of arms. Jed ran his fingers across the iron-plated surface painted in the same ice blue color as their cloaks. In the center was a golden crown with a broadsword running through it. He tested its weight, finding it surprisingly light, yet sturdy.

Slowly, sunlight fell over their campsite, leaving shadows where the darkness once covered the ground. Jed kept expecting Telman to wake any moment, only to find him still asleep.

Something caused his hairs to stand up. Instinctively, he grabbed the shield and held it up. In an instant, he felt a powerful blow against the shield. He caught his breath, then turned the shield to find an arrow lodged in it.

Telman opened his eyes and saw Jed beside him. "Ambush!" he said as sprang out from his blanket, snatching the shield from Jed. He smashed the arrow shaft off and screamed at the Varexians as he moved to cover Kara.

Another arrow flew at the Varexian lookout as he was about to nock an arrow. The arrowhead pierced through his leather amor and went deep into his chest. He fell off the rock in front of Jed. There was no time to react.

"Protect the girl," Telman ordered the remaining Varexians. With shields like Telman's, they gathered around her and formed cover. Meanwhile, Telman ran behind a boulder, searching for their enemy.

"Nobody move!" he ordered.

Jed ignored him and ran over to the dead Varexian, grabbing his bow and quiver. The wooden frame was simple compared to those his family used for elk hunting. Another arrow skimmed his shoulder as he dropped to the ground.

"Get out of there!" Telman said. "Find cover."

Jed didn't move. He sighted a figure amid a boulder field ahead, concealed between two hefty rocks. His focus remained on the man as he snatched an arrow from the quiver and nocked it in a single motion.

When the figure appeared again, a smile appeared on his face as he fired.

The arrow traveled fast. A second later, the figure dropped to the ground.

Telman was stunned, as were the others. The distance had been almost 200 yards. Before anyone could speak, Jed threw the quiver onto his back and ran across the campsite over to a boulder opposite from Telman.

"We need to move," Telman said, still shocked at Jed's kill. "No scout travels alone."

An arrow smacked against his boulder near his hand. Telman pulled back as he turned to the Varexians. "Leave the girl with the boy. We need to hit them from the side. Jed, can you cover us?"

Jed nodded as he drew another arrow. Telman and the Varexians sheathed their swords, wielding composite bows from inside their cloaks. Kara hurried over to Jed and crouched low against their boulder. She fought back tears as she gazed at the dead Varexian and whispered a prayer. The corpse's skin had turned darker, his eyes now white as his skin had once been.

Finished, Kara watched Jed as he scanned the area with a calm demeanor.

"Where did you learn this?" she said.

Ignoring her question, he scrutinized the rocks for any moment. Hunched low, Telman watched for the enemy as the Varexians headed across the ridge northwest of where the first man had fallen. Telman then joined them as they crept up toward the boulder field. A flurry of arrows pelted them, bouncing off their shields as they ran for a better position and fired back.

Jed spotted three bowmen, their ashen clothes acting like camouflage as they blended among the rocks. They pulled back, while Telman and the Varexians pushed toward them. Their backs were now turned to Jed and Kara.

Then a tall, cloaked figure appeared atop one of the boulders in front of Jed. His dirtied grey clothes had perfectly concealed him until he began crawling across the rock. He now stood on bent knee, lifting a thick long white bow from his side. He then drew a hefty bright arrow from his quiver and aimed at Telman as he ran between rocks.

Jed held a long breath and fired. The arrow struck a few feet from the bowman, who instantly leapt backwards and somersaulted off the rock and behind another boulder. Another arrow in hand, Jed went to run after him.

Kara tried to grab his arm and hold him back. "That's Arthema, Grancaliga's best archer. Don't fight him. He'll kill you."

"If I don't, he'll kill Telman, and then us."

Shoving her hand away, Jed sprinted through the soft snow up to the boulders. His teeth visibly gritted, he moved boldly through the boulder field, as though daring Arthema to shoot. He couldn't explain his intense desire to protect Telman, other than it was what he expected of himself or any soldier.

Seeing one of the enemy bowmen vulnerable, Jed tried to take a shot, but broke off at the last moment to evade another arrow fired from a hidden Arthema. He turned in the direction where it had originated and pursued his elusive foe, eager to close the distance between them.

Weaving through the rocks, he hopped from one to another to get a better view. He fired a shot at the bowmen harassing Telman to distract, then spun around to see Arthema shooting from a kneeled position in the snow. He shot back and ducked. Both missed the other, though Jed now bore a deep cut on the side of his face. But rather than frighten him, he felt more determined than ever. He kept running after Arthema, following his marks in the snow.

Then his footprints ended. Jed stopped.

Out his right eye he glanced at Arthema standing in the open, his bow aimed at Jed. He was like Kara, Telman and the others; deathly white skin, burning amber eyes.

"I now have two heads to bring back," the man said.

Jed desperately tried to think of something that would distract Arthema. If only a moment, just to give him just enough time to fire.

He threw back his cloak hood and abruptly faced Arthema.

The man stepped back at the sight of Jed's foreign complexion, his bow almost dropping from his hands.

"What are you?"

The delay was all Jed needed; he brought his bow up and let an arrow fly before he threw himself behind a boulder. His bowstring taut again with a fresh arrow, he peered around the corner. Arthema's bow was on the ground, a trail of trickled blood leading away.

Suspicious, Jed waited before retrieving the bow, momentarily fascinated with the bone-like material. He then ran back to aid Telman, dispatching the remaining enemy bowmen with an arrow between their shoulders.

Coming out from behind a rock formation, Telman put his bow away and stared at Jed with amazement. He was about to speak, then noticed Arthema's bow in his hands. "You killed him?"

Jed pointed at the trail of blood behind him. "I wounded him, but he's still alive."

"He'll go back for help," Telman said. "We've got to leave now."

Returning to their campsite, they grabbed their belongings. Kara timidly approached Jed to say something, but Telman pushed her along the ridge ahead of them. "We have to get to the passageway before the rest of Grancaliga's men arrive."

Paying brief respects to the fallen Varexian, the band moved at a hastened pace toward the imposing mountain wall ahead of them. South of them, there was the murky silhouette of an army column.

***

Grancaliga maintained a cool disposition as a disturbance broke out at the front of the ranks. Soldiers broke out of formation in pursuit of an unknown target. Concealing his displeasure, his colonels accompanied him as he strode forward alongside the main column. A commotion started ahead. Grancaliga watched as his men within visibility of it went for their weapons, only to refrain when they saw what caused the disturbance.

A minute later, a small group of sentinels approached Grancaliga, carrying Arthema over their shoulders. A broken arrow was lodged in his side. He had a stupefied expression on his face.

When they reached him, Grancaliga dismissed the other soldiers and had his colonels stand between them and the main column. He didn't bother to ask where Arthema's men or his bow were as he waited for him recover and explain himself.

"The ambush was perfect," he said.

"Perfect doesn't fail."

"General, something happened I couldn't have planned for." He gazed up at Grancaliga with a frank vulnerability, wincing as he tugged at the arrow in him.

"Who?" Grancaliga said.

"I don't know. He was…not Forenian."

Grancaliga frowned.

"I've never seen anyone like that," Arthema said. "He was also very skilled with the bow."

Cocking his head to the side, Grancaliga sounded severe. "But not better than you. What does that tell me?"

Arthema he nursed his wound. "General…I have not yet failed you. We can still reach them."

"We will."

"May I return to my post, general?"

Beholding his prized archer with a fatherly demeanor, Grancaliga stood beside him as he rose to his feet.

"You may," he said.

He then pulled a dagger from his hip and thrust it into Arthema's side against the arrow, digging deep. Arthema stumbled, but the general held him upright as he turned the blade inside him. When it finally came out, the blood-soaked arrow fell into the snow.

Grancaliga warded off a colonel who sought to aid Arthema as he staggered in the snow. "His suffering will remind him of his duty."

Pushing through the group, he ordered the column to march at the double quick.

On the next hilltop, he heard cries and iron clashing.

***

"Get down!"

Telman pulled Kara to the snow as they narrowly evaded an arrow from a crossbowman standing on the slope to their left. Behind them, Jed dropped to his knee and fired another arrow. His arms were growing weary, as were his legs. He concentrated on his breathing, keeping his muscles relaxed and loose so they wouldn't tighten up.

Pulling Kara back up, Telman hurried her over to the Varexians. They formed a semi-circle to guard her, their shields on their backs as they all ran down the hill. The heat of the triune sunlight had loosened the snow that now gave way beneath their feet. They dug their heels hard as they kept their eye out for more sentinels.

Jed followed in the back. Ahead, the mountain wall seemed to grow higher and higher as they approached. The solid rock was encased in a solid bluish wall of ice. Icicles hung like spearheads from the edges as though pointing down to the bottom section of the wall, shrouded in a fine but thick mist.

The bow on his back, Jed ran to catch up. He then found himself fallen in the snow. A solid force had knocked him off his feet. He recovered just as an enemy sentinel struck at him with a sword. Kicking it away, Jed drew his short sword and slashed at him. The sentinel parried and went for his chest.

Recalling the same ploy by Telman, he sidestepped then lunged forward, stabbing the man in the neck. The Forenian clawed at the spurting wound as Jed left him.

He came to the bottom of the hill and flat terrain. Another sentinel appeared from the snow with a throwing knife. Jed instinctively raised his sword, knocking it away before it could hit his face. By then, the sentinel had drawn a short sword and charged him.

A brief duel ensued. Jed was clearly the inferior swordsman, but his comparatively dark appearance left the sentinel unnerved as he tried to gut him.

An arrow went through the sentinel's leg, sending him into the snow.

Below, Telman lowered his bow and smiled. "Come."

Sheathing his sword, Jed sprinted across the flat ground and soon rejoined the group. Behind them, they heard a loud rumble of a cadenced march. A war cry fell down the slopes with an avalanche-like speed.

"He's here," Telman said.

By then, Jed didn't need to hear the name. Grancaliga's identity was revealed in how everyone spoke of him.

When they reached the mist, the Varexians slowed their pace. They grabbed their shields and entered cautiously. With Telman in the rear, Kara clung tight to Jed's left arm as they proceeded on a narrow, well-defined path. Unable to see more than a few feet ahead, Jed's ears grabbed at any noise.

Kara breathed heavily until Telman reassured her. "You weren't wrong."

"I do hope so."

The Varexians gasped.

"What?" Kara said. "Did you find it?"

None answered. She shoved herself off Jed and ran through the mist. Jed and Telman followed her until the mist dissipated. Kara stood near the

Varexians, her hands covering her face.

Jed came to her, finding a short glacial bridge spanning a vast chasm below. On the other side was the solid mountain wall of ice. A small but clear opening was at its base.

"We made it," Kara said as another war cry blasted through the mist.

Kara and Jed went first across the bridge, followed by Telman and the Varexians. Jed inspected the passageway. Natural light shone into it, revealing a long, winding corridor.

"Why are we stopping?" Kara said to Telman.

"We have to destroy the bridge," a Varexian said. "If we don't, they'll catch up to us eventually."

"That can't be done in time," Telman said. "It's made of solid ice, and we have no explosives."

"Then what do you propose?" Kara said.

Telman's head hung low. He held a fist against his side, then sighed. He glanced at Jed as if seeking agreement.

He knew that look too well.

"No," Jed said.

"It has to be done," Telman said.

Kara saw Jed's distraught face, the resignation in the Varexians. Biting her lower lip, she confronted Telman. "You can't do this. I need you."

"If we don't, Grancaliga will have you by the day's end."

"I can't do this if you're dead."

The war chants loudening, Telman grew hasty as he spoke to the Varexians. "We need to hold this bridge for at least a day, maybe more."

They all nodded.

"I can't do this on my own," Kara said as she seized Telman's arm. He smiled as he eyed Jed. "You two will go on without us."

Jed said nothing as Kara turned to hide her conflicted face. Telman then took him aside. "You know her importance. Will you protect her with your life?"

Jed nodded.

Telman reluctantly slid his shield off his back, handing it to Jed. "My grandfather's grandfather made this. If I die, I have no heir. I suppose you'll have to do."

He then suddenly embraced the boy. "You'll need it until you can fight without it. If you can, you'll be a true soldier."

Jed stepped back and held the shield with trembling hands. "I intend to prove it."

"Keep Kara safe. Wherever home is for you, chances are she can help get you back there."

Wielding his longsword, Telman waved the Varexians over to the front of the bridge, where they formed a solid shield wall. He stood behind them, directing Kara and Jed to the passageway.

"No matter how long it is, don't stop until you reach the Field of Baldae," he said. "Look out for each other."

Her cheeks wet, Kara hugged Telman. "But without you…"

He shoved her away. "Now go. Go!"

Kara went to Jed at the mouth of the passageway. His stoic look embarrassed her so that she wiped her tears with her cloak sleeves. It wasn't until she walked a few steps ahead out of sight that Jed did the same to his own moistened eyes.

***

Grancaliga strove to the rows of soldiers bottling up the path, his colonels close behind. At the front, sentinels maintained a shield wall covering the ledge between them and the bridge leading to where Telman and the last Varexians stood defiantly. The snow on both sides was imbedded with arrows, a dozen corpses strewn on both the bridge and on Grancaliga's side.

"General," Telman said. "Something you lost?"

Grancaliga couldn't hold back a smile. He addressed a sentinel. "How long have they been there?"

"Not sure, sir."

"Did you see the girl when you arrived…or a strange-looking man?"

"No."

Grancaliga then noticed one of the bodies. It seemed familiar. He turned it over with his heavy boot.

Arthema; a long deep wound ran across his chest.

"He died fast," Telman said. "As will the rest."

Enraged, several bowmen took aim at him. The arrows bounced harmlessly off the Varexians' wide shields. Their eyes conveyed a newly found confidence behind tightly fitted helmets.

"What do we do?" a colonel said.

"Wait," Grancaliga said as he withdrew to the back. The soldiers who heard him were baffled, as were the colonels hurrying after him.

"Sir? We don't understand."

"Neither of us can leave this spot. We wait until they must or make a mistake. Perhaps the girl will turn back."

"What if she doesn't?"

Grancaliga laughed as he glanced back at the mountain wall. "Telman wants to die. Far be it from me to appease him."

CHAPTER 4

Jed walked behind Kara as she moved briskly through the passageway. The space was narrow, though wide enough for them to stand side by side if she had wished. The ceiling went high up, the icicles hanging from the top like bats. Jed watched them warily as they turned a corner, his new shield close to his side.

Every now and then Kara stopped for a while. Then she would sigh or glanced down at the manuscripts before heading off at an even faster pace. Her demeanor toward him gradually began to grow cold and aloof.

"I hope you keep up," she said as if speaking to herself. "That shield is quite heavy. Telman could carry it, but he's had to bear it since childhood. He's a great warrior, though he'd never admit it. He feels like a failure, but he has no right to think that about himself."

After a distance, they came to a place where the walls seemed to melt. Jed touched it and though frigid, it was as solid and dry as glass window. Kara resumed her hasty stride when Jed was about to pass her.

"We shouldn't have anything to fear here," she insisted. "The map says we pass through the mountain wall and then reach the Field of Baldae. We'll have to go through it before we reach the Hercerla Forest, and then finally the Temple where..."

She went mute and glanced back at Jed, still walking. "I meant to say that we still have a long journey ahead of us. As I said, I hope you're quite up to it."

Jed offered a neutral expression. "I'm in good shape."

She was about to speak, but the words fell apart on her lips. A minute later, she blurted out her thoughts. "Why are you helping me? I know I saved you, but you don't owe me for it. Grancaliga isn't interested in you. You don't have to come with me if you don't want to. He'll let you go."

"I promised Telman I'd look after you."

"I just don't understand how Telman could leave me like this. I don't understand why he chose you to come instead. I…I just…"

Her words once more failed her, and she stomped a foot angrily as she turned back to face the passageway. When Jed caught up with her, she initially looked at him with displeasure. She sighed resignedly as she wiped her eyes again. It would have been easy to get offended by her remarks, but Jed didn't feel anger from her. It was fear.

From there, the passageway became long and straight for several miles. The sky became grey. Dry snowflakes fell like tiny cotton balls. Their hoods back on, they kept going as the powerful wind tore at their clothes. When it subsided, Kara sat to take off her boots and rubbed her feet as she took small bite from a bread loaf in her pack.

"I made plenty of it," she said, offering Jed some.

While she rested, Jed further examined Arthema's bow. He was still amazed by its simple yet elegant design. The material was as smooth an elephant's tusk, yet it could bend while maintaining a sturdy frame.

"At least you're competent with that," Kara said. "I hope it won't be necessary, but you never know."

Jed offered her his short sword.

"Thank you, but I'll be quite alright," she said. "I'm not a warrior. My power is reading and the occasional potion brewing. A few recipes are only found in the texts. It was so wonderful to be able to replicate it. To think the same potion someone made a thousand years ago still works. I was so excited when I first made one…I was so worried then about keeping it all a secret, until I found out how hard it was to convince someone who can't read that you can. Only Telman believed."

She touched Jed's arm as she showed the bundle clasped to her belt. "If these texts are lost, it will be as if our history and our age of kings never happened. Grancaliga wants to destroy anything that reminds our people of the past."

"Evil men seemed to be the same here as they are in my world."

"The greatest symbol of that is the crown. It's at the castle where I live, near the keep built into the mountain summit. But the ancient entrance to the mountaintop where it's located is sealed by a powerful spell."

She opened one of the texts and gently pointed at a page before closing it. "Only I know how to open the door. Not even the heir to the throne knows."

"Where is he?" Jed asked. "Why hasn't he joined you?"

"He's in hiding."

After thinking about it for a moment, Jed asked Kara, "Does Telman know where this heir is?"

"He does. But he'll die before he tells Grancaliga…and that's what frightens me."

***

In the morning, they rose and continued through the passageway. By then, the sky had partially cleared and one of Forenia's three pale moons was visible between the cracks in the mountain wall. Powdered snow slid off the walls and whirled around like sawdust as they turned a corner and felt a warmer breeze.

Kara earnestly ran ahead, with Jed trying to match her speed. It had nothing to do with endurance or stamina. He was used to heavy packs, but the weight of his equipment was uneven. He kept readjusting the belt on his tunic and shield on his back until it all felt more comfortable. He had his bow in hand, an arrow in the other as he got close to Kara as possible before her pace quickened.

Gradually the snow on the ground dried up as the last moon above brightened for a while and then faded out in the greying sky. Streaks of light shone down before vanishing entirely. Jed was at first hesitant to pass under them until Kara read one of the texts and marched through.

They turned around the bend, and then Kara immediately stopped. Looking over her shoulder, Jed saw ahead the mountain wall's end, the exit a large tunnel-like shape. What lay beyond was obscured and vague.

Kara anxiously rushed toward it, while Jed proceeded with a vigilant glance to their sides. Standing beneath the exit, she put a hand to her mouth.

Jed reached her as she turned to him. "We're here."

Together, they left the mountain wall and stood on a ledge overlooking the Field of Baldae. As far as he could see in every direction were seamless prairies of withered golden grass. On the horizon, rolling black clouds noiselessly billowed as though caught in a tempest. Dotting the landscape in the distance were fortress-like boulder formations, while seared leafless trees stood like hollowed scarecrows with feeble blackened arm-length branches hanging over the grassland. All that could be heard was a faint windless wail like the sound of a seashell close to the ear. The lukewarm air held a strange aroma hinting of bittersweet memories. No animals or creatures of any kind could be seen.

Exhaling loudly, Kara consulted the map for a long time, ignoring Jed's inquiring look.

"We must head west," she said. "There's no path or route. We just have to keep going."

Tersely stuffing the map in her cloak, she climbed down the ledge. Jed scanned the vicinity, uneasy about the grass fields. There was no telling what could hide within and stalk them. He had no intention of walking into another ambush.

When they came to one of the trees, Kara peered at it curiously before turning to the texts. After reading a passage to herself, she wiped her eyes and resumed her pace as though nothing had happened. Jed took only a brief glance at it, hardly catching the indecipherable words carved into the trunk.

As they walked, Kara spoke abruptly to him. "I know you're better with the bow, but you might consider conserving those arrows. We don't know how long the journey will be. Or perhaps you can...oh, never mind."

They came to another steep ledge. Taking the rope Telman had given him, Jed tied it to a firm edge and tested its trustworthiness before forming a knot around Kara's belt. He handed her the rope and instructed her how to properly rappel down. When she was too timid to do so, Jed took it and demonstrated it himself. She insisted on holding onto him as he brought them down together. He did so, then climbed back up to retrieve the rope before scrambling to a spot where he could safely leap down.

Kara gasped in horror as he landed in front of her and dusted off his knees. "You shouldn't take risks like that. We can't have you hurt. I don't know what I'd do. I suppose I'd...well, you just can't get hurt."

They waded through the grassland, passing by more barren trees with decayed bark and crumbled exterior offering an ominous appearance.

"Forenians once passed through here," Kara said. "That was a long time ago."

The sky offered no indication whether it was midday or evening. They rested by a rock formation as tall as a single-story house. Jed took out his short sword and practiced some of the techniques Telman had taught him, first without the shield and then later adding it to his training. Kara silently read from the texts, frequently pausing to watch him whenever he had his back turned to her. Later, they moved to one side of the rock when the air grew cold.

Listening to the distant wail, Kara stared blankly at the prairies before them.

"I don't understand," she said. "Why am I doing this?"

"Huh?"

"I meant why *me*. There were others who could have done something. The council, generals, thousands of others who had more power than I could ever dream. All gave up. So why *me*?"

"None of them could read," he said.

Kara considered his words as he spread out their cloaks as beds and went to make a fire. While trying to start it, he realized he still had his pocketknife with him, which included a spark-magnesium igniter. When he sat down, Kara moved slightly to give him space beside her.

"I wondered what it was like when my people first crossed here," she said. "Now I think I know. I'm proud and ashamed. Forenians then must have been very brave. What happened?"

She observed Jed as he balanced his sword in his hand, then planted it in front of him.

"Telman said you come from a military family," she said.

Jed nodded.

"It seems you hope to continue that. What does your father think?"

For once, Jed was withdrawn.

"Your father doesn't trust you?" she asked.

"He thinks I'm not ready. I'm going to prove I am."

Kara rested her chin on her knees as she leaned forward. "I wasn't meant to read or write. I had an older brother who was supposed to, but he died young. My father never taught me, but he didn't stop me, either. Only males were scribes. Maybe that's why nobody believed me, except Telman. I suppose that also kept my secret safe, too."

The next day, they trekked across a small hillside and tried to travel as far as they could without rest. They found themselves sleeping that night on a hillside that looked no different. The next day, a similar situation occurred. Day after day, it was the same ledge, the same grassland and dead trees.

Kara made no comment on it at first. After the third day, she anxiously checked the map, then the texts. At night, she would reread the same passages to herself, recite the same verses and prayers.

"It can't be like this forever," she said. "There would be something here telling us about it. All it says is that Forenians first crossed the Field because they had a great faith in what they saw, though it's not clear what that means."

One evening, she didn't read anything, her head in her hands as she stared into the campfire. A soft cry rustled through the prairie grass. Unlike the continuous wail they had grown accustomed to, it had a human-like quality.

Drawing his sword, Jed moved to the side of the hill and looked down.

"What is it?" Kara asked.

Jed didn't move or speak. He couldn't think of any words to describe what he saw.

Kara hesitantly approached him and turned her eyes to the scene below. A large winding line of specter-like creatures moved across the fields. In their cloaks, they appeared to be Forenians, but there was an uncanny aura around them. Their movements were fluid and smooth, as though the ground moved beneath their feet. The indiscernible cry did not seem to emanate from their lips.

"Who are they?" Kara said. "What are they doing here?"

Jed gently took her arm and led her back to the campfire. "I'll keep watch," he said to her as he gestured to her makeshift bed.

"What if they attack?"

He shrugged. "Having you awake won't matter."

Kara pressed her lips together. "I can't fight with a sword, but I know the old prayers. You don't think it's what kept you safe when Arthema attacked?"

"I guess then you can pray if you want."

With a scowl, Kara prepared to get in her bed, then with a sigh got up and offered a prayer of protection from the texts.

"I'll skip the sleeping potion tonight," she said as she pulled her cloak over her chest. "If I'm going to die, I'd rather be awake and prepare for it."

Jed's voice was firm. "You won't die."

"You're quite confident in your abilities."

"Would you prefer I not?"

Several minutes later, the campfire had died down so that Kara's face was a mere silhouette. She spoke in a whisper.

"I miss Telman…but I'm glad you're here."

***

The cry continued through the night. The creatures were still on the move when Jed and Kara departed in the morning. Despite the lack of sleep, Jed felt well rested. A rationed piece of Kara's bread helped restore whatever energy he lacked.

Jed took them northwest for a while and then moved back to their original route. But they realized that wherever they moved, the creatures seemed to change their path as well.

Meanwhile, the moans went on until Kara pressed a hand against her chest and nearly broke into tears. Breaking from Jed, she drew closer to the creatures before stopping to study them. Now able to make out their features, it appeared they were Forenians. But Jed couldn't overlook the strange glow around them.

"I understand them," Kara said. "They're speaking in the old tongue."

Jed strained his eyes as he studied their agonized faces. Their mouths indeed moved, their lips conjugating words he couldn't comprehend.

"They're in pain," she said as she listened carefully to their speech. "They're lost and pleading for help…they were trying to cross the Field and didn't make it…now they're caught between our world and the next…yet they don't seem to realize we're here."

Her eyes brightened. "We should try calling them." She was about to, but Jed put a restraining hand on her.

"What's wrong?" she said. "They may have been here for a long time. Maybe they need help like we do."

"How can we help them? We don't even know if we're going the right way."

Kara bit down on her lower lip, glanced at the crowds longingly, then joined him. As they moved, the crowd turned in their direction and for the next day maintained a parallel course. Their unremitting pleas for deliverance tugged and wrenched at Kara's heart, but Jed could not ignore the soulless, doll-like gazes that recalled the only time he'd seen his father draw his gun, during an encounter with a homeless drug addict.

That night, Kara was animated as she perused the manuscripts. Her small finger tapped a page as she brought it over to Jed.

"It's the Prayer of Revival," she said. "It can bring people back from the gap between the two worlds. If I recite it, that could restore them."

Tossing a twig in the fire, Jed scowled. "There's no pointing endangering ourselves."

"I have to do something," Kara said. "I can't just sit here and watch them like this. I've seen too many of my people suffer already."

"We need to look after ourselves."

Her reaction made him step back from campfires flames that now matched the brightness in her eyes. She sprang up from her seat and stood in front of him, her voice uneven and broken. "Well, what would you know? You can't read the texts. I can see why you wouldn't care. They're not your people. You'll never know what it is like to see them in agony and feel their pain. There's a connection between Forenians, and you don't have it."

She calmed only to wipe her wet cheeks and looked away from Jed. "There's been enough suffering. If I won't help them, what am I doing here? What are you doing here?"

Puzzled when Jed offered a sympathetic look, her face softened as she put the manuscripts by her bed and then climbed into it. She didn't seem to be speaking to Jed any longer. "Am I wrong to want to help them?"

"They don't want help," he said.

***

Jed awoke to the sound of Kara singing at the bottom of the hillside. He hastily looked at her bed. The manuscripts were still there. A terrible feeling settled into his stomach.

Snatching his things, he ran down to meet her.

With her arms extended wide, her eyes closed as she raised her chin high and sang the prayer from memory. Her joyous face and melodious voice had a hypnotic-like effect.

In front of her, the phantom-like beings gathered in an unorganized mass. Though they listened, their expressions offered no hint of emotion. Their ears seemed trained on the words themselves. When she was finished, she opened her eyes and gazed hopefully upon them as if awaiting their embrace.

The agonized faces instantly turned to rage. With weapons drawn, they raised a battle cry and charged at Kara. All that saved her were several arrows loosed from Jed's bow, striking down the first wave of enemies.

Kara ran back toward Jed as he continued firing. A few took shots in their side, glanced at their wounds, and pushed forward.

"They're wraiths," Kara said. "The undead spirits of ancient Forenians."

Jed aimed at one of the heads and let fly another arrow. It plunged into the wraith's head as it dropped, its complexion growing dark. Grabbing Kara's hand, he led her over to another hill and kept her at the top.

With only a handful of arrows left, he drew his shield and short sword as he charged down the hill and threw himself into their midst. When the first one attacked, he sidestepped and thrust hard, slaying them in a single stroke. He immediately turned and blocked a blow with his shield, dropping to his knees as he cut at their legs.

Realizing he would soon be surrounded, he ran back up the hill, then pivoted back to strike a wraith in the head. As he continued fending them off, he noticed their bodies disintegrated shortly after their deaths, only their clothes remaining.

He soon had to change tactics to counter those could strike him from a distance with longswords. Running to Kara, he had her retreat to a boulder formation as the wraiths overwhelmed their campsite. He switched to his bow again. The wraiths did little to avoid his aim as he struck one after another until only a few were left. Unwilling to use up his final arrow, he reverted to his short sword and went on the offensive. Their swordplay closely mirrored Telman's. Anticipating their strikes, he delayed his move until they had extended themselves, then closed in to ram his sword into their gut with both hands. As they collapsed, he pulled a bloodless sword back and watched them pass into the next world with an eerie sense of relief on their faces.

Hearing Kara scream behind him, he turned. The wraith held her in his arms, a bone-hilted longsword placed against her. The rotting creature carried himself with the same leader-like demeanor as Jed's father whenever he spoke to a subordinate.

Throwing down his shield, Jed held his short sword high and gestured at the wraith. The phantom sized up the boy, then laughed with an undead voice. "You think you can beat me? I am Melakia, the greatest swordsman Forenia ever had."

Kara's eyes widened. "You're the one who led the rebellion here as our people crossed. You tried to turn back to the forest. Why are you doing this?"

"Because you all betrayed us."

He went to slay her, but Jed had already gone for his final arrow. Shooting wildly, he then dropped the bow as he raced to protect Kara. Melakia moved to avoid the arrow, while Kara slipped out of his grip as she threw herself toward Jed.

Melakia tried to strike her down, but Jed blocked him and kicked him back. With his far-reaching sword, Melakia kept Jed at bay while the two paced around each other. Bringing the sword down to his side, the phantom swung up hard, knocking Jed's sword away. He then slashed down with a powerful motion. Jed rolled to avoid the hit and struck back. Touching his chest, he felt a painful sting as blood trickled down his hand and tunic.

Grinning, Melakia offered a theatrical demonstration of his sword skills as Jed retrieved his weapon. His heart beat violently in his chest, and his instincts told him to panic and flee. Anything it seemed was better than death.

But he couldn't run, even if he were allowed to live. There was only one choice.

"Are you ready to die?" Melakia said.

The specter-like being grew alarmed as Jed smiled.

"No," Jed said. "I'm just beginning to live."

***

The duel went on as the sun gradually dropped and hovered just above the horizon. Melakia's fighting style was completely dissimilar to Telman's. Jed prevented most the blows from striking him, but gradually more and more cuts ran across his chest, then his arms. He held his sword lower and lower until he could lift it only to defend himself. Though his fate seemed all but sealed, he refused to believe it. He would accept it when it came, not before.

Finally, Melakia knocked the sword from his hand and struck him again in the chest. Unable to hold himself up, Jed dropped down and crawled away on his knees. He heard Kara crying in terror.

"Watch out!"

Jed rolled to the side, seeing the longsword sink into the grass. Crawling on the ground, he came across an arrow where a corpse had once lay. Snatching it, he returned to his bow. Kara screamed again, and as he turned with the bow in hand as he saw her fleeing Melakia down the hill.

Struggling to his feet, he stared at the arrow. He then remembered his pocketknife still with him. Taking it out, he flicked the igniter, glancing at the dried grass with intrigue.

"Help me!" Kara screamed.

Plunging the arrow into a clod of dried grass, he positioned the igniter against his bow. Pulling the arrow back as hard as he could, he flicked the igniter until sparks lit the grass. He peered through the ball of flames at Melakia, who had now caught Kara and held her close.

A desperate glimmer in his eyes, he fired high.

As he brought the bow down, he saw the side of Melakia's neck erupt into flames that soon spread across his entire cloaked body. Kara fought him off and ran. After a few feet, she realized the hem of her dress was on fire. Falling, she tried to put it out, but like with Melakia, the flames spread swiftly.

Jed arrived and tore at the hem, pulling her away as the material reduced to a black heap. A little way from them, Melakia's cloak had done the same. His body had already vanished.

Wiping the dirt from her face, Kara breathed rapidly. She tried to weep when she saw Jed's wounds. "Oh, you're hurt."

Jed gasped, leaning on his side. He felt lightheaded, his vision blurred and foggy. She helped him up to recover his gear and with great struggle brought him back to the campsite. Laying him near the fire, she went to her cloak.

"The manuscripts…they're gone."

She searched her cloak, then examined the area around the campsite. Covering her face with her hands, she fell to her knees and sobbed.

"What have I done? This is all my fault. I've undone everything."

Jed muttered as he gestured feebly to his side.

With a held breath, Kara flipped over his shield. Tucked within the handles were the texts. Clasping them once more against her belt, she took Jed's hand and held it in hers.

"Bless you. They would have destroyed them all."

Jed opened his mouth but couldn't speak.

Kara kissed his hand, gazing back at the weapons scattered across the field.

"What you did just now..."

Jed could hardly hear her. Drifting in and out of consciousness, he felt the blood flow from his wounds. He should have thought it was odd Kara merely stood over him as if waiting for him to die. But the pain stifled all thoughts until he slipped out of awareness. He felt a sense of falling, and for an instant, he prayed he was waking from a dream.

***

"Jed, wake up."

He opened his eyes expecting to find his mother standing by his bed. Instead, it was Kara, and the Field of Baldae still surrounded him.

"Are you alright?" she said.

Jed mumbled as he sat cross-legged on his cloak. He then pulled back his tunic and gasped as he touched his chest, feeling no pain there or anywhere else on his body.

"You're healed," she said, coming alongside him with a thimble-sized glass container. "It's a special potion that was brewed a long time ago. It restores a person completely, no matter their condition. My father gave it to me. Only one batch was made; the recipe didn't even have a name. Just one drop left now."

"Thanks," Jed said.

Kara put the potion away as she offered him bread. "Please forgive me. I didn't...I thought I could help them. I'm just tired of...being alone..."

Neither one of them felt like traveling that day. They sat and talked as the prairies grew dark the sky lit up with bright stars that flew like starships across their view. Some stars formed constellations and pursued others like warriors in combat.

"I don't understand," Kara said. "I was bringing them out from the gap between our worlds. It's an awful place. Why did they turn on me with such hate? How could Melakia call *me* a traitor?"

She tore off her headscarf and held it in her lap as her eyes shimmered. She used the headscarf to dry her cheeks, then put it back on.

"Why do you wear it?" Jed asked.

"It's a sign of submission to Forenia's heir."

"What do the men wear as a sign of submission?"

"Swords."

Jed rose and without speaking went to the place where Melakia's corpse had fallen. Sifting through the remains, he retrieved the bone-hilted longsword and its skeletal sheath. He brought it back to the campsite and placed it by his bed. It was nearly double the length of his short sword, but weighed less. A sense of pride overcame him as he cradled it in his lap; it wasn't just a weapon of war. It was a symbol of what he had done, of what he could do.

"The manuscripts said a rebellion occurred during the journey from the forest," Kara said. "Melakia gave up trying to reach the Perelor Mountains. Others believed him. But I didn't realize those wraiths were *them*. I presumed they had gone back to the forest. Maybe they couldn't find it. But perhaps that's why they hated me...I'm living proof they were wrong. It's the same thing I saw in people's eyes when I lived in Merce Haelle. They seemed defeated."

Jed found her sitting beside him, her head rested against his arm. "Why am I alive now? Why wasn't I born when Forenia was united and strong? Why was I destined instead to watch a twilight kingdom fall into total darkness?"

The questions were eerily similar to those Jed had asked himself in recent months. Since he was a child, he had been steeped in the family history, how his forefathers had fought under American heroes like George Washington, Stonewall Jackson, Teddy Roosevelt, and George Patton. To the Hayes, wars and their cause didn't matter so much as how the man conducted himself; brave in the face of death and faithful toward his brothers-in-arms no matter what.

Yet the face of war, and the nation itself, had since changed and become thoroughly ambiguous. Jed kept his discomforts to himself and away from his family, but in his heart, he too wished he had been born to an earlier generation where such confusion did not exist.

"I'm afraid—afraid we'll never find the forest," Kara said. "We've traveled for so long, yet it seems we've gone nowhere. I fear we're missing something. Is there a clue in the text?"

"What does it say?" Jed said.

"Only what I said before: they crossed the Field of Baldae into the Perelor Mountains because they had a great faith in what they saw. But what did they see that we haven't?"

"Maybe they didn't see it with their eyes."

Kara looked off contemplatively. "We just keep walking?"

Jed nodded. The side of her head buried deeper into his arm.

"I never thought of that," she said. Her body moved away for a second. "Will you lead us tomorrow?"

"Yes."

"I hope Telman held them off a long time," she said.

✳✳✳

Grancaliga stood up from his seated position overlooking the glacial bridge where Telman and the Varexians maintained a seamless shield wall. The rest of the army had pulled back waiting for further orders.

"I don't want them at ease," Grancaliga said to his colonels as he pointed at the troops. "Have the men in the front remain alert; the others can reequip and bring more supplies from the rear."

"Sir, it's been less than an hour since we first arrived, and at the end of a forced march."

"I want nothing to encourage Telman and his friends, to give them hope we might withdraw."

"How long do you plan to wait?" a colonel asked.

"Telman doesn't know how to quit. But he doesn't know how to win, either."

A colonel grew bold. "Perhaps we could end this quickly if you were to lead the attack."

Grancaliga considered it, then shook his head. "Telman wants us to do that. He wants to go down fighting. Whether brave or reckless, it's clear his greatest fear is that we will take him alive. At the same time, he's not eager to die. Nothing stops him from attacking us."

"Why?"

"We won't know if he is killed."

Moving between the ranks, Grancaliga approached the ledge near the bridge and studied Telman. The man paced back and forth near the passageway with his longsword rested against his chest. He avoided Grancaliga's powerful stare until all others there took notice. Standing among the Varexians, Telman finally acknowledged the general with a frustrated glare.

Grancaliga nodded. "When I finally catch up with the girl, I will most certainly want him alive."

CHAPTER 5

A small breakfast was made for Jed when he got out of bed. The rest of the campsite was also packed up. As he ate, the two of them looked out at the prairieland. Though it was the same landscape they had seen every morning for days, Kara hurried Jed to renew their trek.

"I feel anything is possible now," she said.

They walked through the grass fields and by the scarecrow trees and boulder fortresses and under the blackened clouds that never offered rain. That howling wind seemed to speak to them, telling them to go back. Kara brought her head up higher and smiled as she glanced at Jed while he searched hard at the hillsides flanking them. No more wraiths were seen or heard. He sensed that they had passed the worst of it.

"It's not quite scary anymore, is it?" Kara said. "Have you ever seen anything like this in your land?"

"Sort of. No wraiths, though."

"It's so strange. When we first came here, I wondered how a place so desolate could exist. Now it doesn't bother me. Maybe it's because I know we won't be here forever."

They traveled for another two days. On the third, they moved through one of the prairies when Jed stopped in his tracks.

"What is it?" Kara asked.

Jed put a finger to his lips, then looked around.

"I feel it now," Kara said. "Something's here."

Jed took another step forward. With his arm extended, he pushed his flat palm out in the air, as if searching for something. He then jerked his hand back instinctively.

"Are you alright?" she said.

Jed kept staring ahead, perceiving unseen energy in the air. He put his hand out again, taking another step forward. A long breath fell from his mouth as he lowered his hand and motioned to Kara. Standing beside him, they took a step together as though walking off a cliff.

In an instant, the Field of Baldae was gone. Before them was a vast and dense forest, the air sweet and clean. Though it was dark, Forena's three satellites shone with such brightness that felt as clear as day, their rays of light piercing through the heavy fog that permeated everything so that the trees seemed to glow.

Kara clung to Jed's side as she looked upon the twisted, warped tree trunks bent over like an old man, the curved branches plunging into the dark, soft soil. She walked a few feet away from Jed, studying the trees before turning to a marked page in the texts. She then snapped the book shut. Solemn, she prayed for a moment as Jed watched quietly.

"The Hercerla Forest," she said. "My people's first homeland. We may be the first here in over a thousand years. There were no others living in the forest."

She became distraught. "What if someone has come since?"

Jed drew his bow and held it by his side. Kara consulted the texts again and then brought them to Jed. "It says the Impora is inside the Ansele Temple my ancestors built in honor of Forena. We have to find our way through this forest to reach it."

"Anything else?" he asked.

"The histories say there may be ancient Varexians still guarding the temple. They descend from Forena's warrior priest class. However, not all of them left when our people departed. No one really knows why they stayed. The text isn't as clear as I would like…after this, you'll want to go home, I imagine."

"Yes."

"There is a prayer that might have been written for you. But it requires Impora's powers. Once we get it, and stop Grancaliga, we can get you home."

Jed thought he heard something move. He quietly prepared an arrow as Kara kept talking.

An animal cry resonated from among the trees.

"That is not the prayer of woodland spirits," she said.

Jed saw something coming from behind. Before he could turn, the beast swooped in with the speed of a falcon and grabbed Kara before running away. It then stopped and faced Jed. He was wide-eyed as he gazed at the werewolf standing on its thick hindlegs, Kara held in its arm-like front legs. Its fur was black with streaks of red and blue running from the base of its neck down to its tail. There was a human quality to its facial expression conveying an agonizing pain that seemed to give it life.

The werewolf summoned three companions from the trees with a howl. He licked his lips as he spoke to them. "At last, you can feast on flesh again."

The trio threw their heads back as they howled. The leader disappeared with Kara, while they began encircling Jed. With controlled breaths, he attempted to keep them all facing him, but they moved too fast. He fired at the one nearest to him. The werewolf tore the arrow out from his fur and tossed it aside as it flashed dagger-like fangs.

Drawing a tinder-wrapped arrow from his quiver, Jed lit the tip and loosed it at the same werewolf. The beast dodged it and snuffed the fire out with a deep, heavy breath.

"Your weapons are pitiful," it said.

The werewolf then lunged at Jed. His shield came off his back just in time. Claws scratched and tore at it, but the iron-plated frame stood firm. Jed struck with the shield, pushing the werewolf away just as another attacked. His short sword got caught in its jaws, and he fought to wrestle it out. The werewolf released its grip and threw its claws at him. He rolled and hacked at its hindlegs, drawing blood. Wounded, the monster roared but moved behind the other two.

"You'll pay for this, intruder," the wounded one said. "We'll let you live as we consume you, piece by piece."

He felt no fear, not because of some great courage. He simply could not fully accept that it was all real, and a part of him believed were they to get him, he would wake up from a deep dream.

The two unharmed werewolves leapt in the air together above Jed. He raised his shield once more, but the impact knocked him down. They went for his legs, but he kicked the beasts before they could sink their teeth into his flesh.

He tried to raise his sword, but one of them ripped it from his hands. Sniffing at Jed's leg, the werewolf salivated.

"Time to feed."

As it went to bite off his foot, Jed frantically yanked the longsword from his back and with a loud cry brought it down hard with both hands. The werewolf blinked at him, then dropped as its body split apart.

The remaining two werewolves jumped back in shock. They howled sadly at their fallen companion, then turned their black eyes on Jed and ran straight at him. Striking from high twice more, Jed then lowered his sword as he stared at the two lying dead together. When he turned to the third, he found it was no longer a werewolf, but a well-built man dressed in brightly colored embroidered military garb. On the clothing was a crest featuring a wolf surrounded by trees, bordered by the same red and blue color on their fur. Moments later, a similar transformation occurred with the other two.

He inspected them closely and found thick scale-like chainmail underneath their garb. Removing it from one of them, he put the chainmail on beneath his tunic. It felt weighty, but didn't impede his mobility as he had expected.

Gathering his things, he went to where the werewolf who had taken Kara last stood. Noting the tracks, Jed followed them closely as he moved through the forest.

Beyond sight, he heard the far-off sound of wolf howls. Taking a deep breath, he trudged onward. Terror sought to grip his heart, but he knew that to give in would be to condemn Kara. He would not fail her, or Telman—even if they never saw each other again.

***

Telman heard a terrible roar as he woke up from his spot against the mountain wall. Grabbing his sword, he felt a blast of wind, followed by a blinding whirl of ice and snow. Throwing his hood on, he stood ready for an attack, calling to the Varexians in front of him. No one replied.

Wiping his dry mouth, he moved through the gust toward the ledge. Before he could see his men, a dark, imposing figure emerged.

Telman immediately went to attack. In one incredible stroke, a great sword knocked his weapon from his hand back into the passageway.

Grancaliga appeared, a large smile apparent. "You thought you could stop me? Better yet, you thought your pathetic band could withstand my powers?"

"Delay was more like it."

"You hardly succeeded."

"When they have Impora, you'll feel different."

Grancaliga approached Telman, his great sword held in readiness. "You and I know they'll never find it."

Telman laughed. "Have you read the manuscripts?"

"No one can read them—except the girl. She'll know the Divinity Prayer."

Telman glanced at the Varexians unconscious near the ledge. The mist dissipated temporarily. The bridge had been obliterated. A rope in hand, Grancaliga tossed it over the ledge to the other side, where a soldier snatched it and tied it down. One by one, soldiers began a deliberate crossing.

"Why destroy it?" Telman said. "Your entire force can't possibly make it across."

"At the Battle of the Five Lagoons, I lost my entire navy in the morning. I still accepted a surrender that evening. My entire fleet was easily rebuilt, as will this bridge."

"You waste your time. The girl will never deify *you*. She'll die first."

Grancaliga chuckled. "I don't doubt it. She wouldn't do it to save her own life. But I have a feeling she will do it to save *yours*."

"You're wrong."

"You're not very convincing."

Telman took a small knife from his hip, pressing it against his abdomen. His chest rose and fell rapidly. "Is this more persuasive?"

Shaking his head, Grancaliga gestured at the Varexians behind him. Soldiers had crossed and now stood watch over them.

"They won't enjoy the swift death you pretend you're willing to take," the general said.

Before Telman could respond, Grancaliga confronted him and kicked the knife out of his hands. "Give up your pretenses. You won't kill yourself. Why, I don't know. My only concern is bringing the girl back. To that end, you'll live."

***

The woods were indistinguishable from one place to another. He moved from tree to tree, anticipating its grotesque limbs to come to life and strike him. The flesh-like bark and the thin trunks planted like a kneeling man left him unnerved. Apart from the howls, something there seemed to speak to him in a multitude of small whispers. The forest teemed with life that could be felt within him but not seen.

The tree stands widened as the werewolf's tracks abruptly stopped. Jed looked out and before him were the ruins of a great stone edifice. Its roof was gone, its outer walls fragmented. Thick vines crawled up and down both sides and wrapped around the pillars like serpents. A large flight of moss-layered stairs led up to an entrance where the wooden doors had rotted away.

At the bottom of the stairs were two werewolves sitting like watchdogs. Their ears perked as they saw Jed approach, but to his bewilderment, they withdrew as he grew close.

Ascending the stairs, Jed slowly walked through the concave-shaped entrance. Though moonlight still shone down into the wide, vast interior, it felt as though he were encased in a tomb. On the walls behind the crawling moss were ornate carvings lined with green foliage, and along the transept, there were stone sculptures of cloaked warriors on small platforms with sword and shield in hand, their features eroded by time and elements. Chiseled into their armor was the same crest embroidered on the wolfmens' garb, all defiled by large claw-size scratches.

Behind a pillar head, he spotted a werewolf, this one standing upright. It growled hostilely at him, but did not move.

"What do you want, intruder?"

He tried to keep his voice firm. "The girl."

The werewolf chuckled. "You're quite the arrogant one. Our master awaits you in the temple's inner sanctum."

The werewolf pointed at the end of the chapel at an interior walkway. Jed looked out the corner of his eye and didn't move.

"If we wanted to kill you, we'd do it now," the beast said.

Jed raised his longsword, gripping the bone hilt with whitened knuckles as he prepared to strike. The creature nodded, then barked reproachfully to werewolves attempting to sneak up behind him. However, he kept his guard up as he entered the dark and musty walkway. It wasn't long before he came out the other side to a smaller space. The ground was littered with fallen spires and crumbled archways. Unattached columns rose to support a nonexistent ceiling. Climbing across the debris, he saw an unmarked doorway above on a broken ledge, absent of any green. Nor were there sculptures or wall carvings.

Throwing his rope up, he secured it and then climbed up to the ledge, entering the sanctum.

A door appeared behind him and closed, a bolt sliding across on its own. In front of him in the circular room was a stone platform where the werewolf leader stood near an altar with Kara bound beside it. The religious and historical texts were on a wood table by the altar. The werewolf silently studied them with knitted eyebrows.

Smiling, it left the table and with an amused tone spoke to the boy. "I am Skollgard. Whoever you are, you're not one of us."

Skollgard licked his lips and ran his claws through Kara's hair. "But she *is*. Oh, that's right. The beast who speaks to you now has the spirit of a Forenian in him, a Varexian no less."

"How?" Kara said.

"We refused to go when all others did. Then the days grew short, and disappeared completely. Now it is only night, forever. The moonlight transformed us. It was so long ago; I cannot remember what I once looked like."

He brought Kara's face close to his. "I want that complexion again, to have eyes that radiate the Spark, not darkness. With you, it can be done."

"You can't read the texts," Kara said. "Varexians were never taught."

"I know the ancient Forenian rituals performed well before those manuscripts were written. Before there was even the written word. A time when our people were 'primitive,' yet strong and proud."

Taking a ceremonial knife from the table, Skollgard placed it against her neck. "To assume my old form again, a sacrifice must be made." He gestured at the altar. "You will perform that role quite well."

"My blood can't wipe clean your crimes," she said. "You're cursed because you broke your vows to the king."

"We stood against him because we knew our people would grow weak if they left the forest. Judging by what I see, we were right."

Jed jumped on the platform. "Let her go, and I'll let you go."

Skollgard noticed the longsword. "That was Melakia's. How did you come to possess it?"

"Fight me and I'll show you."

Skollgard hesitated before unleashing a fiery howl that shook the room as he raised his claws toward the moonlight, as if drawing power from it. Wielding a curved sword from his side, he eagerly approached Jed.

"I'll sacrifice your worthless corpse as a burnt offering," he said. "With that sword, I'll remove your heart."

The words flowed automatically from Jed's mouth. "Come and take it."

Skollgard unleashed a rapid series of strokes aimed for Jed's center, and he countered each and drove the wolfman back against the altar. Moving around the room on all fours with the sword in his mouth, Skollgard broke into sprint and lunged at Jed's throat, then rolled to the side and cut at his leg. Jed barely evaded the tip as it tore at his boots. Off-balance, he was unable to fend off a powerful blow against his sword and stepped backwards.

Spinning around, Skollgard brought his sword down and across Jed's chest. With a loud, agonizing cry, Jed dropped to the floor in agony as Kara wept in despair.

"You may have killed Melakia," the werewolf said, "but I was always better than he."

His black eyes widened as Jed picked himself up and raised his longsword, pushing back the jarring ache in his chest. His tunic was torn through, revealing the scale-plated chainmail still intact.

"You survive only by stripping my men of their things," Skollgard said. "Just like you fight with another man's sword."

Jed offered no words before throwing himself back into the fight. Skollgard barely kept one step ahead of the boy. Emboldened by his short recovery, Jed found within himself a renewed strength. He was frightened by his own boldness and aggression in the face of death by such a fearsome enemy, and yet in doing so, he felt some deep barrier within shatter, unleashing a part of himself he had never known.

"Why are you willing to die for her?" Skollgard said. "What's she to you? You're nothing to her."

Jed stabbed hard, twisting his longsword. He violently shoved the hilt guard against the opposing blade, pushing Skollgard down the platform.

"You're both here for Impora, aren't you?" the mutated Varexian said. "Have our people fared so poorly they must return here, where they should have stayed? Are there no more Forenian men that their women must turn to a stranger?"

Ignoring the taunts, Jed kept up his offensive. Skollgard's actions grew wild, frantic. In desperation, he called to his minions in the other parts of the temple. They burst through the sealed door and set themselves upon Jed, wrangling the longsword away from him as they ripped at his chainmail.

Skollgard tossed his sword to the side and approached Kara as he and the other werewolves began chanting.

"We shall become men again, brothers!" he said with outstretched hands.

Jed pulled out from the pack, leaping onto the platform. Deprived of his longsword and shield, he drew the short sword from his side. Skollgard face became as white as Kara's as he stared at the small blade. His voice was solemn. "Where did you get that?"

Jed said nothing, perplexed as the other wolves whimpered and slowly backed away.

"Fool," Skollgard said between gritted teeth. "*You* will never be king."

The fallen Varexian prepared to plunge the knife into Kara's heart. His hand raised in the air, he became still. His facial features contorted as he struggled for breath. Blood dripped from his quivering jaw.

He looked down at his chest, where Jed's short sword had sunk deep. Wobbling back and forth, he fell against the altar and attempted one last time to slay Kara before dropping to the floor. Jed wasted no time grabbing Skollgard's blade and striking down the remaining wolfmen still stunned by their leader's demise.

Kara got off the altar and pleaded with a dying Skollgard. "Where is Impora?"

The werewolf flashed his sharpened teeth a final time as he let out his gasping breath.

"You'll never find it."

Kara held back her tears as she looked over at Jed leaning against his blood-soaked blade. She knelt beside him while they watched the corpses gradually revert to their human form. Skollgard proved to be a tall, sturdy man with long hair, lying beside the altar with the short sword still in his chest.

Kara averted her gaze for a moment before impetuously kissing Jed on the cheek.

"Thank you," she said.

Initially astonished, over time a smile appeared on his face. He hadn't known quite what to think of her, what he thought of her, until then. They both tried to voice their feelings, but each time they went to speak, the words dissolved on their tongue.

"How much more will this go on?" Kara finally said. "It's more than I can bear. These were my people."

"No more than I."

She lowered her head. "I know…and that's all right…there's nothing wrong with who or what you are. You've been as brave as any Forenian warrior would ever hope to be. But it is different when they are the same people as you. They're supposed to care for you. They aren't meant to fight you. When they do, it's like a brother or sister or a cousin betraying you. That is all I've ever known. That's why I hope for a king again. Yet it seems like everyone fights to prevent that from happening. They would rather die. What is it they fear so much?"

Jed looked down at Skollgard's curved blade by his side to find it transformed into a majestic-looking longsword. He brought it back to the man's corpse and placed it across the body, then laid the clay-cold hands over the hilt.

"Won't you take it?" Kara said. "You took Melakia's sword,"

Jed got off the platform. "Some are best left alone."

He led her out of the inner sanctum as she took a final glance at Skollgard's body, now adorned in his temple guard ceremonial tunic.

"What is it?" he asked.

"He got his wish."

Moving through the chapel, Kara consulted the texts as she looked about. "Skollgard's lying. The Impora simply *must* be here. But of course, it's impossible to follow anything written in the manuscripts. They describe the temple as it *was,* not as it is *now.*"

They searched several cloisters outside the chapel. The silence now pervading over the temple felt more unsettling than the wolf howls or the winds blowing through the Field of Baldae. Placed against the wall were more stone sculptures, the broken heads lying at the feet. Vines cracked through the floor and ran the full width of the walkways.

"You think there might be more of them?" Kara said.

"If there were, they would have come before."

"That's good, in several ways. It means we're safe, for now. It also means only a few Varexians refused to go with the king. You're probably wondering why my people didn't take Impora with them when they left. You see…the spirit of Forena dwells in this place. Only certain people can wield it. The king at the time either did not take it or was not capable of it. When our last king died, it was foretold that only Impora had the power to restore the monarchy. For everyone but my family, it's been a dearly loved myth, but nobody believes it."

A shy smile fell across her face. "I suppose I should count myself blessed. For a thousand years, others in my family read the prophecy, but never lived to see it. I get to witness it with my own eyes. I get to know for sure it's true. All they had to go on was faith."

She was about to step ahead, but then pulled herself back and allowed Jed to go first. "Maybe you might understand the text, as you did before." She recited a passage chronicling the Forenians life prior to their exodus from the woods, their life in the fortress city of Derla Haelle. Jed raised an eyebrow and shrugged curiously.

"Maybe we should go there."

"You think there might be clues there?" she asked as she closed the book. "I know the way."

They departed from the temple ruins and took a path between a long row of trees. The leaves continuously covered the ground, yet the branches were full. There was a weak but peaceful humming sound coming from all directions. Kara's dangling hand occasionally brushed against Jed's as she sang a prayer, delighted when the spirits replied with the same melody.

"The woodland spirits," she said. "They are like those in the Perelor Mountains. They won't harm us, provided we do not desecrate or defile the woods. Skollgard and his men must have been prudent to avoid offending them. Then again, that may have been what caused their transformation in the first place."

Jed listened half-heartedly, reliving his fight with Skollgard again and again. Something had changed in him. It was as though old instincts carried through generations that had long kept dormant inside had at last awakened. His chest swelled with an intense confidence he found difficult to control, reassuring him no one could stand against him.

The path continued for several miles until the woods ended with a clear demarcation. A few steps ahead there was a large wall encircling the city of Derla Haelle. The gate was still secure, but sections of the wall had crumbled. The pair hurried to the breach and climbed through it. On the other side, they found dilapidated homes and shops and other structures. The streets were strewn with rusted weapons and overturned wooden carts.

The muddied ground was rough and thick.

Kara stood in the center of the street, closing her eyes as she breathed deeply. Her long hair flapped in the wind as though she had gained flight. Avoiding the mire, she made her way up the road toward the prominent stone keep in the center of the town.

"This was the king's home," she said as they reached the tower. She read more to Jed from the manuscripts, allowing him time to consider it.

"We're trying to find Forena's Crypt, where Impora was laid to rest after he carved out of wood the first of our people," she said. "But the entrance to it wasn't where it's supposed to be. You think the king's tower might tell us?"

"We can check."

The tower door was ajar. Keeping Melakia's longsword sheathed, Jed held the short sword in one hand, Kara's wrist in another as they went through the great hall where a tall throne stood against walls engraved with illustrations. Kara studied the carvings while Jed searched the throne. Finding nothing, he moved up the damp, moist stairway and rifled through each room until he was at the top. The king's quarters were austere and plain. Few things had been left to examine. No books or signs of writing tools, not even a desk. All he came across was a worn banner in the corner with the same sword and crown symbol as that engraved on his shield. Intrigued, he wrapped it and carried it amongst his gear.

Heading down the stairs, Jed rejoined Kara in the great hall. She too had come across nothing that offered them hints of where the entrance was.

"We could have missed something in the temple," she said. "Now that Skollgard and his men are gone, we should be able to search it more thoroughly. Unless we want to look through more of the town."

Exiting the tower, Kara froze.

A tall figure stood before them, another Forenian. His eyes glistened as he smiled at her. His voice left every hair on Jed's skin standing.

"A pleasure to finally meet you."

Jed reached for his longsword, but stopped when he saw a dozen bowmen behind Grancaliga.

"How did you get here?" Kara said.

"The same way I broke your Varexians outside Merce Haelle when they had twice my numbers. I dream of a united Forenia, and I will it to be so."

"You couldn't possibly have navigated the Field of Baldae on your own."

The ominous man appeared fascinated. His hands behind his back, he drew close and ordered his men to lower their bows. He pointed at the manuscripts in her arms.

"I know you can read," he said. "I saw your pen and paper in your room."

"I'll never tell you how to open the crown room," she said. "You'll never get it."

"The crown interests me, but that is not the only thing I want. Those books you hold contain more than histories or legends of the past. Spells and prayers that can beckon the gods, or make a man one."

She tried to protest, but his self-certainty stopped her as she lowered her head.

"Oh, yes, young one. I know. I truly *know*."

Grancaliga finally acknowledged Jed's presence. "So this is the outsider I'm supposed to fear? I expected a man, not a boy."

His men became restless as they collectively noted Arthema's bow strapped to his back.

"I confess I'm impressed," Grancaliga said of Jed, though he addressed Kara. "I commend your ability to make it this far alive, without Telman."

"Where is he?" she asked.

Throwing back his long flowing cloak, Grancaliga stepped to the side and displayed Telman and the Varexians bound and on their knees.

"Must I explain further?" the general said. "Or is my proposal not obvious?"

Kara looked at Jed and whispered. "If he gets the crown, he'll destroy it. I'd rather die than have that happen. If I recite a certain prayer over him in the right setting, he'll become a god."

"I won't play God, if that's what you're asking."

"It's your life at stake, too."

"I'm here to protect you."

"You won't if you're dead."

She turned to Telman. The Forenian seemed unharmed, but exhausted. He gave her a strange look that made her eyes moist. Without looking down, Jed felt Kara's hand place something in his. He tucked it in his belt.

"They'll all be spared?" Kara said to Grancaliga.

"Yes. Even this outsider, who should pay for killing Arthema. A small price in the end."

"Why should I trust you? Why would you willingly let them live?"

"What difference will it make if they're free? Can they stand up against a god? Do they think they'll find the heir to the throne and restore the monarchy? Did you find Impora in the temple? No. It was a wonderful myth. Your courage is notable, but it's time to accept my inevitable reign."

"We've seen plenty of your reign wherever you conquered."

"Those I slaughtered died for less offense than your little group here. Do not provoke me."

"Don't give in," Telman said.

Grancaliga drew his great sword and struck Telman in the shoulder. Kara screamed and tried to reach him, but Grancaliga pushed her back. "A minor wound. He'll live, but only if you come with me. Make your choice now."

Closing her eyes as she turned away from Telman, she nodded.

"Good," the general said. "Now hand me that dagger."

Pushing back her cloak, Kara withdrew the knife's edge from her side and hesitantly gave it to Grancaliga. He led her back to the ranks, ordering a colonel to set the Varexians free.

"And Telman?" Kara said. "You promised."

Grancaliga's icy stare seemed to wound Telman a second time. He then ordered his binds cut. "Better you live to see how pointless your stubbornness was. I am eager for the day you finally accept that Forenia is mine to control."

Telman was quiet as he staunched the flow of blood from his shoulder.

Kara gave Jed a longing glance before vanishing within the military column as they marched away from the city ruins. Jed watched them until they reached the forest before he approached Telman. He wasn't afraid. The desire to fight was just as strong as before.

"It's good to see you alive," Telman said to Jed. Ensuring Grancaliga and his men were gone, he sighed as he called the Varexians to him. "I feared Kara wouldn't make the trade."

Jed frowned as the older man chuckled. "There are more things at hand than you realize. I sent you with Kara and stayed behind for a reason. I would not leave these men, and Grancaliga wouldn't have spared you. Even if he had, I figured Kara wouldn't trade her life for yours...though based on what I just saw, I'm not so sure."

"This was always your plan?" Jed said.

Telman rose with the Varexians' help. "There are things I know that aren't in the manuscripts. If Impora is real, you won't find Forena's Crypt in the Ansele Temple as it is."

"How then could Kara and I have found it?"

"You wouldn't. *This* has been my plan since we reached the mountain wall. Grancaliga wouldn't kill me if he knew Kara would surrender for my sake. Had we not delayed them, we wouldn't have reached the temple at all. The only reason we got here at all is because of Grancaliga's powers."

A Varexian spoke. "What if he is deified?"

"Then Impora is our only way to stop him," Telman said. "It's not too great a hope, but there never was much, I suppose."

They traveled to the temple ruins. Telman spoke in a strange tongue as though reciting a poem, with his eyes closed and hands high. As each word fell from his lips, sections of the outer wall noiselessly appeared, followed by the pillars and then the ceiling. When he was finished, the entire temple was restored to its former glory.

"The crypt will be easy to find," Telman said to Jed away from the group. "But I am in no condition to fight, and my men's spirits are too low to face this challenge head on. The only counsel I can give you is this: the legend says only a man who truly knows himself will be able to defeat the spirit guarding Impora."

Taking out his longsword, Telman offered it to him. "Will you go?"

Jed accepted the blade and, without remark, began walking up the steps.

"Why are you so willing to fight?" Telman said.

Pausing, Jed turned back. "Do you believe Impora will be there?"

Telman smiled. "I hope it is. Just as I hope you'll return with it."

"I will."

CHAPTER 6

Jed entered the temple as though arriving for worship service ten minutes late. As he looked around, he wondered for the first time since he had arrived in Forenia whether it was all a dream.

The room felt as large as the Field of Baldae. White chandeliers hanging in the air were like constellations below the dark vaulted ceiling. Tall narrow stained-glass windows adorned the clerestory, yet no light shone through. The stone sculptures were now restored, their features uncannily humanlike. He stopped in front of each and studied their defined faces like they were his own ancestors.

On the walls, carved illustrations told stories, the skyward narratives running up toward the clerestory where the stained-glass windows concluded each tale.

After wandering for what seemed an hour, he proceeded down the nave. The sculptures, with their dignified but severe expressions, seemed to guard the space against violence.

The entrance to the crypt was a modest door near the right-side aisle. The curved stairway lit entirely with mounted torches led him down farther than he was prepared to go, but he didn't stop. The air was dry and clean, the limestone-like walls glistening as though new.

Opening another door, he entered a large room partially lit by a handful of torches. No columns held up the ceiling. Carved out of the walls were sculptures of men, each with a crown on his head and a ceremonial sword. On the other side of the room was a platform with a towering sculpture of a cloaked Forenian, his hands extended outward with a fatherly demeanor. On the platform was a plain-looking sword. Between it and Jed was a wide canal full of unknown liquid, a narrow bridge leading to the other side.

As he approached the bridge, a shadowy figure appeared near the platform. The demonic being had a fragmented appearance, sections of his body and tattered cloak missing. His broad hood covered the upper section of his partial face. With two gloved hands, he held a longsword facing the ground.

"I've come for Impora," Jed said. "Stand aside. Everyone ese who has fought me has lost."

The figure spoke in a hushed voice. "I will not."

"What is your name?"

"Whatever name you give me."

Jed looked down and finally noticed the armor-clad skeletons scattered around the room. Each had their own sword run through them. They had been defeated, but he had no fears he would join them.

"You killed them?" Jed asked.

"No. They killed themselves."

"Why?"

"Fight me, and I'll show you."

Grasping Telman's longsword, Jed ran across the bridge and threw an overhead attack against the demon, who parried the blow and struck back. He then threw himself into a relentless attack, overtaken by a state of forgetfulness in which all hesitation was purged.

Compared to his duels against Melakia and Skollgard, his performance then would have ended both fights within moments. But the demon proved a far worthier opponent. His strategy was dissimilar to Jed's, and each found themselves desperately fighting their way out from the corners and with the canal to their backs.

Jed had never appeared more self-assured. He almost laughed as he knocked the demon to the ground, slashing at its ghostly arm. Though no blood poured from the wound, the demon shrieked and fell back. A second later, Jed achieved another hit on the same arm.

Drawing away, the demon then counterattacked and with the very tip of its sword sliced through Jed's shoulder. He winced, but kept fighting. He missed a parry and received another cut on the upper arm.

Ignoring the pain and the dripping blood, Jed circled the demon and maneuvered him to the bridge. Lowering himself with bent knees, he held the longsword at his side and swung up hard, knocking the demon's weapon away. A short thrust struck him in the chest. Another echoing shriek rattled his ear as the demon floated back toward the platform.

"Give up, now," Jed said. "I'm unstoppable."

"I'll give up when you do."

"I'll never give up."

"Then neither shall I."

The demon feinted a swing to the head, then brought his sword down. Jed was too slow. Another spot on his upper shoulder was now red. Crying out, he lunged forward. His attacks grew more ferocious. The demon time and time again avoided a killing stroke to the heart.

"What is it you fear?" the demon said.

"Not you."

The voice sounded so certain. "It is something else. I can sense it."

Jed swung from high to the right, but the demon dodged it and kicked him back.

"Your father," the demon said. "You're afraid you won't live up to him, or your grandfathers before him. You're afraid you'll never live up to them."

"No."

"That's why you're so bold. You'd rather die than yield. It would be courage, if only what you dreaded was the failure to do what is right."

"That's why I fight."

"You fight because you're terrified of not being what you think someone wants you to be. But who are you? Do you even know?"

Jed gritted his teeth. "The one who defeats you."

With the demon on the opposite side of the canal, Jed lowered his sword. The demon did the same, appearing just as wearied. Panting, Jed waited to catch his breath before speaking.

"The sword is mine."

"It will be mine, or no one's."

"I won't end up like these dead men."

"We shall see."

The battle persisted beyond what Jed thought he was capable. His arms gradually became weary, but whenever he saw the demon's limbs still nimble, he regained endurance. Something about it seemed to demand every ounce of effort in him. Thoughts of his father also spurred him on.

The two traded wounding strokes until Jed's wet tunic was scarlet red. The blood felt warm and poisonous on his skin, yet every time he was tempted to despair, he saw the demon move slower, its blows weaker against his blade. He might have slain the creature then, had his agility and power not also been drained by wounds and exertion.

Offering one last assault, Jed met the demon in the center of the bridge and clashed, their hilts locked together as one. They pushed their weight back and forth as they stared into the other's eyes. Though the demon's face was murky, the two amber eyes glowing back at him reflected his face as clearly as a mountain range on serene alpine water.

Twisting his hilt, Jed shoved the spirit back, then drove his sword into its side. A terrifying screech fell from its formless mouth as it frantically brought its sword hard against Jed's chest. The boy's hilt reduced the force as it tore through his flesh. Nearly brought to his knees, Jed remained upright as he watched the demon also struggle to keep his footing.

Placing the tip against its heart, Jed held his sword with bent arms.

"Yield."

"I will never surrender."

Jed did not strike. The demon's pale eyes had no spark, yet there was no hate in them.

"You think you won," the demon said. "But you won't get what you seek from me."

"Why do you fight me?"

"You attacked me."

Jed's mouth opened slightly as he deliberately brought his sword down and away from the demon. It occurred to him that for the first time, he had thrown the beginning strike.

The ghostly figure did not move as Jed grimaced at the bodies near them, then sheathed his sword with a heavy breath. His arm quivered as he extended his hand toward the demon.

"I do not want to kill you," he said. "Somehow, we must both use the sword...if you're willing."

The spirit paused. Its movements seemed drawn out as Jed anxiously watched it raise its sword, then place the weapon back into its scabbard. A quasi-invisible hand reached out and accepted Jed's gesture.

"I am willing."

In a flash, the demon became a beam of light. When it faded for an instant, Jed stared at the figure shaking hands with him. The being with a mirror-like reflection stepped toward him and dissipated into a formless essence before seeping into his body. A cooling sensation raced through him as the blood vanished from his clothes and his wounds were healed.

Ahead, the large stone sculpture was gone from the wall. It now stood as in bodily form before the platform. His eyes were like a furnace that drove out all darkness and shadows from the room as he raised his hands.

"Come," he said.

Jed approached. The man's aura compelled him to kneel in reverence. His heavenly voice echoed through the room.

"I am Forena, who with Impora created the people of this realm. I commend you for your actions. You have resisted your inner demon. With such courage and virtue, you have shown yourself worthy to bear my sword."

Taking Impora from its platform, he held it in his palms as he lowered it before Jed's face. "With this, I can return you to your home world. Or you can bear it in my name, but I cannot assure you shall live. Speak the word, and I shall do it."

"I stay."

"Such a swift reply. Why?"

"I'll never be the man I want to be if I leave now."

Smiling, Forena held the sword high. Around them, the crowned sculptures' stony exterior softened as they took a human form. Each holding a scepter in one hand and their sword in another, they formed a semi-circle around Jed. With soft voices, they chanted the same cryptic words Telman had used to restore the temple.

"The kings of old are here to bear witness," Forena said. He then placed the blade in Jed's hands. Despite its mundane appearance, he sensed its full power as he wrapped his fingers around the hilt.

"Help the rightful heir reclaim the throne of Forenia and unite the realm," Forena said. "But remember this: *Whosoever bear this sword shall it wield.*"

"I will remember."

"Good. Now receive my divine blessing."

Placing his hand on Jed's head, Forena spoke urgently in a strange tongue. An indescribable current flowed through Jed as the kings' chant turned to shouts. The force surging within him became so intense he cried out, but the effect doubled again and again until finally he felt his spirit passing into another realm.

✴✴✴

"Is the girl ready?" Grancaliga asked as he approached a colonel standing outside her door inside the royal castle. He wore his formal dress uniform, his large boots glistening from a recent polish.

The colonel nervously opened the door, then waved the general in. He entered to find Kara gazing out the window. She wore a red ceremonial dress that perfectly matched their eyes. The lengthy hem fell down her, stitched with gold. A front section of the dress once featuring the Forenian royal crest had barely visible stitches, and the patch replacing the crest was hardly noticeable.

Kara faced Grancaliga, a distant air about her. He avoided commenting about her beautifully braided hair. Getting her to wear the dress had required enough effort.

"It's time," he said.

She said nothing as she looked back out the window.

"You gave me your word," Grancaliga said. "I will hold you to it."

Kara sniffed and wiped her nose as she turned around, her eyes directed at the floor.

"What if I decide I won't?" she said.

"Then you will be responsible for what I do next. Think well of what that might entail."

"I am ready."

She was headed for the door when Grancaliga stopped her and pointed at the manuscripts lying on the writing desk. "We must not forget those."

Outside the door, an escort of 20 soldiers awaited them.

"How shall we get there?" Kara said.

"We are to walk," the captain of the guard said.

"Is the weather fair?"

"Quite."

Four of them accompanied Kara as she walked behind Grancaliga, who was flanked by six men on each side. The rest followed, proudly waving his personal standard. They moved to the upper castle level and to the tower until they reached the top. There, the mountainside merged with the tower as though one had come out of the other. The procession moved toward the summit, where a large stone door bearing the royal crest blocked a passageway.

When they reached it, Grancaliga ordered all to a halt. The guard then stepped away from him as Kara was brought to the door. Opening one of the manuscripts, she came to a page and stammered. Grancaliga glared and was about to protest, but held his words.

"Take your time," he said.

"Why so gracious?" she asked.

"I am a cruel man, but it is out of necessity, not pleasure."

"It makes no difference to me why a Forenian betrays his people and the throne."

The soldiers and colonels all grew tense. Those standing near Kara stepped back slightly. The general eyed them, then smiled at Kara. "If you prefer, we can stand here for a while until you decide to honor your word. In the meantime, I'm certain my men and I have no qualms marveling at your beauty."

With pursed lips, Kara moved to the door and began speaking. She recited from the manuscript for over a minute. The royal crest on the door lit up as the stone creaked and cracked and dust flew into the air. It slowly swung outward on its ancient hinges, revealing a darkened path.

Lighting a torch, a soldier went to approach the entrance, but Grancaliga took the torch and led the way with Kara behind him. Ducking beneath the doorway, he moved quickly through the passageway until they reached a small room. The soldiers all came with lit torches that fully brightened the room.

In the center was a stone slab with the Forenian royal crown sitting atop it.

No one moved for a while. Grancaliga smiled broadly as he stepped up to the slab and delicately picked up the crown. Facing his men, he held it high above his head.

"The era of the monarchy long came to an end," he said. "We shall now make that evident to all."

He almost dropped it as he spotted Kara running through the passageway, having slipped through the ranks. The crown in hand, he raced ahead of his men out the mountain and onto the tower. A look of terror fell across his face as he saw Kara stand on the parapet; the other side leading directly to the bottom of the castle.

Her legs shaking violently, Kara sobbed as she glanced behind her. "I won't deify you! I'll die first!"

Grancaliga first restrained his men from any brash action, then held his hands up. He walked as close to her as he dared. "You don't want to die."

"Only if living is worse than death."

"If you fall, our history will be forgotten. Even if someone somehow learned to read."

"You intend to destroy it, anyway."

"No. I plan to build a future unshackled by outdated institutions and disunity. That has been my dream since I was a child. Everyone mocked it. What could the son of a commoner ever do? But I had the will to achieve it, to build a more perfect, unified Forenia. That's how I conquered armies twice the size of mine. I never lost the will."

"The will to dominate."

Grancaliga held the crowd in front of her. "What does this trinket represent, if not that?"

"Responsibility and duty. That's why you would destroy it."

He stared at her, then tossed the crown at her feet. "Come down from the wall, and it will be given to you for safekeeping."

She seemed disgusted. "After all you've done to get it, the lives you've taken and cities you've razed, you want me to believe you'd just hand it over?"

"Before, no. But what difference does it make if you deify me?"

"Then there's no reason for me to accept your offer."

Grancaliga chuckled. "I will certainly destroy it if you choose the alternative. And then I'll take out my wrath on this castle, this city, and all the inhabitants in it. Their lives are in your hands. Are you truly willing to sacrifice them for a few moments of moral self-righteousness before death?"

Taking in the full breadth of Merce Haelle below, Kara wiped a tear from her eye, stepped off the parapet, and hastily picked up the crown.

"I keep my word," Grancaliga said. "You should be more trusting."

"I trust you to be what you are. That's what I fear most."

Running a hand through her hair, he brought her close to his side as he led her back to his men.

"I want the ceremony done as soon as possible," he told a colonel. "Are the preparations finished?"

"Not yet. We're following the instructions the girl provided us as best we can. But…"

"What?"

"How do we know if she is telling the truth?"

"If she was willing to let this entire city be exterminated, she would have taken the leap."

"I see. Everything should be ready in a day or two."

"Make it one."

Escorting Kara with her arm forcibly draped over his, Grancaliga led her back into the castle and to her room. "You must wear that dress for the ceremony. I like seeing you in it. I'm sure that boy would have, were he here."

"If you're determined to also get an heir out of me, know this: I will take the leap first, whether it dooms the city or not."

He violently seized her, kissing her hard before he pushed her back into the room. She panicked while he remained in the doorway.

"The thought hadn't crossed my mind, until now," he said. "And to be honest, I'm content to be a god. Then I'll require no heirs from you or any woman."

He slammed the door shut, bolting it. As he left, her cries moved through the door and resonating down the passageway.

***

Telman and the Varexians walked slowly toward the temple as Jed emerged from the entrance. Jed strode down the steps, and by the time he reached Telman, the older man had dropped to one knee, the Varexians anxiously following his lead.

"It's me, Jed," he said timidly.

Looking up at him with wide eyes, Telman and the others rose. He would have spoke, but Jed raised a hand. He then brought out Impora and displayed it. The Varexians quietly gasped.

"You did it," Telman said as he wiped tears from his eyes. "It *does* exist."

Detaching Telman's longsword and scabbard from his belt, Jed knelt before him and handed it back.

"You saw Forena himself?" Telman said. "What did he say?"

"That I should help the heir to the throne take it back. I figured it would be easier to do if he had his sword again."

The Varexians eyed their leader, who folded his arms and smiled. "How did you know?"

Jed took the tattered banner from his belongings and gave it to Telman. "From the king's tower. The same crest on it as your shield. The temple ruins also had some occupants who recognized your short sword."

Admiring the banner, Telman ran his fingers over the delicate cloth before handing it to a Varexian. He urged Jed to stand.

"I see you're waiting for an explanation," he said. "Kara and her family had their long-kept secret. Mine did, too. Perhaps that is why we understood each other so well when we first met. Both of us bear burdens over matters that happened before our time. My family couldn't read the texts, but the royal family preserved its oral traditions, legends, and spells. I long desired to reveal the truth. I couldn't understand why we would not assert our rightful claim. But my father forbade it. He said the time wasn't right, that by maintaining our silence we would survive. I didn't believe him, until I served on the Elder Council and saw what he had endured for years. I maintained that silence even as I watched the Varexians I was supposed to lead as their king get slaughtered."

"It was not your fault," a Varexian said. "And we still have a chance."

"Yes, a chance; more than a chance, now that we have Impora. Are you ready to use it?"

Jed nodded.

"Kara will no doubt be held in the royal castle," Telman said. "Grancaliga will hold the ceremony on the tower, along the mountainside. What better way to mark the beginning of his rule?"

"How will we get in?" a Varexian asked. "The castle's easily defended even with the small garrison that surrendered. Grancaliga must have a large force inside it now, not to mention an army that can take the field."

"We sneak in, then."

"Rescuing Kara won't restore your family to the throne," Jed said. "Grancaliga must be destroyed."

"How can we accomplish this?" Telman said. "That sword is powerful, but can it take the place of thousands?"

A strange smile formed on Jed's face as he brought them to the forest tree line. With Impora raised above his head with both hands, he pointed it at the vast woodlands. The blade glowed as a beam of light streaked through the air and shattered into countless small pieces, falling like embers onto individual trees.

The ground rattled as the woodland spirits fled the forest and gathered around Jed and his companions. On the trees, the leaves fell and faded out of the sight in the air, while the bark dried into thin flakes and seeped into the soil. The limbs tore themselves from the ground as the trunks turned to torsos. Twigs became swords and their branches transformed into arms encased in chainmail. Roots pulled up and gained feet as one by one marched toward the Forenians until in the place of the forestland was an immense army clad in heavy armor and brandishing all sorts of deadly armaments.

One of the soldiers came to Telman and knelt, raising the visor to his thick helmet.

"What are your orders, my lord?"

CHAPTER 7

Grancaliga sat on the wooden throne as the great hall filled with soldiers prechosen to participate in the deification ceremony. His long gray cape spilled down from the throne onto the steps before it. His colonels stood in a line down and to the side of the throne, their armor and uniforms without blemish. In the windows overlooking the city, a great noise emanated from the streets as the rest of the army prepared to celebrate as soon as the proclamation was made following the ceremony.

Looking around the rows of banners and flags hanging from the ceiling, Grancaliga frowned for a moment before summoning a colonel. "Where is she?"

"In her chambers."

"Bring her to me now."

The hall grew quiet as the colonel left in haste. All looked at Grancaliga as he listened to the cheers ascend from the city and through the castle windows.

The colonel returned with Kara behind him and escorted by four guards. Every eye turned to her. She wore the red ceremonial dress as before, her hands covered in matching gloves that went up to her elbows. However, her hair was now unbraided and covered by an ice blue headscarf.

The other colonels gave him a worried look, but he offered them no reassurance as he stood from the throne and came down the steps. Everyone bowed, save for Kara. The manuscripts in one hand, in the other she held the king's crown.

"Why did you bring it?" Grancaliga asked.

"The same reason you brought me here."

"I didn't go through all that trouble to find you so you could make me king. I've fought too many campaigns to destroy it."

"We'll see."

He laughed as he stroked her feather-light hair. "I won't let your feeble attempts to provoke me spoil the evening. Once I'm deified, it won't matter. When I become a god, none can resist my will."

Overcome with fervor, the colonels threw up their fists as they hailed Grancaliga. Their passion swept through the hall as the soldiers joined in praise of their leader, the air filled with rattling spears and swords

"It is with this devotion I triumphed," he said to Kara. "Imagine then what it will be when I am a god. I will make Forenia greater than it has ever been, its armies feared by any invader that might arrive. We will become a united people again. You soon must choose what place you want to have in it."

"Wherever there is someone willing to oppose you."

The high-pitched sound of a war horn bellowed outside in the distance. Grancaliga pushed Kara away from him as she dried her lips still wet from his kiss. He approached a window and gazed out beyond the city toward the hilly plains surrounding it. He could hardly make out the silhouetted single figure along the horizon mounted on a white horse.

A courier rushed into the great hall. "Sir, our watchmen say the rider bears the royal standard!"

"Varexian?"

"No, the king's banner."

"I had them all burned."

He noticed Kara breathing heavily.

"It's Telman," he said.

"How could he have returned so quickly and without one of our scouts spotting him?" a colonel said as they looked out the window. "And where would he have retrieved that standard? He didn't have it on him when he found him."

Grancaliga was quiet for a while as he studied the lone rider, then Kara as she avoided his gaze. He lowered his head. "I win a hundred battles, a dozen campaigns, and not once did I make a mistake until now."

"How, sir?"

"I had the heir to the throne in my hands, and I not only let him live, but go free."

"Telman? He can't..."

Their leader gestured at Kara. Her face seemed to settle their doubts. Another blast from the war horn sounded through the city and sent a slight tremor through the stone fortress. Gradually, the hilltop filled with more riders until they formed a single rank across the plain.

"The man must be insane," Grancaliga said. "He comes at me with a few dozen horsemen. Does he think he can take the city, let alone the castle?"

He turned to a colonel. "Gather a vanguard of cavalry, divide them into two groups, and then send them through the city's side gates. At the same time, have a company of pikemen in reserve come out the front gates. The vanguard will flank them from behind and push them toward the city, where the pikemen will block any escape."

"What of Telman?"

"If convenient, have him brought here alive. Killing him will be my first act as a god. A fitting thing, if he is indeed heir to the throne. What better way to mark the end of kings?"

A minute later, the castle drawbridge lowered as a thick column of horsemen strode out into Merce Haelle, splitting off in opposite directions in the city grand center led by standard bearers holding Grancaliga's banner. Behind them marched pikemen, the glint of their spears like jewels in the night's sky.

"Come, my dear," Grancaliga said to Kara. "You must watch. It is the first time you will have seen my perspective during a battle: the side of the victor."

She held herself at a distance with arms crossed, but her eyes switched back and forth from the plains to Grancaliga, his hand comfortably wrapped around his warrior belt. He allowed her to pray without interruption.

"You noticed the marks on it, I see," he said as he tugged at the belt. "Some keep track of how many they've slain. A man in my position must either find something else to track, or enjoy collecting belts. I only remember the great ones I've killed, the worthy ones who impressed me. The ones who deserved to die at my hand.

Kara was silent.

"You're wondering whether I will include a mark for Telman on it," he said. "But in truth, I've been more curious about your foreign companion. Would the boy be worthy? We'll never know."

"I already know."

He waited for her to go on. When she said nothing else, he chuckled. "Even if he is with Forenia's 'heir,' he won't enjoy the scrap of mercy Telman might receive."

The two group of Grancaliga's horsemen had departed the city and vanished into the darkened countryside, while the pikemen advanced to the front gates and moved across the field toward the hillside. There, the king's standard remained in place, as did all the riders on its flanks.

"What are they waiting for?" a colonel said.

"Telman wishes to die with honor," Grancaliga said. "He wants to face the enemy head on. Commendable, but foolish."

Behind the king's standard, a commotion arose, as though Forenia itself groaned. Then a horseman rode up to Telman and handed him something. His steed reared as he stood up in his saddle, holding aloft Grancaliga's banner.

The general reacted coolly, crossing his arms as he called to his colonels. "We may need reinforcements."

Blowing his war horn a third time, Telman drove down the hill, his sword held high as the horsemen behind formed an arrow-like shape. They charged toward the pikemen, who quickly gathered into a tight shell-like cluster.

A dozen or so war horns then thundered. Infantry appeared on the hillside and raced onto the plain. Wave after wave swept the field until they covered it like a wave of blackness.

"Sound the alert," a colonel said to a courier standing in the hall's doorway.

Converging on the pikemen, the heavy swordsmen hacked away at their foes' spears, cutting them down as Telman drove through the center. Within a moment, the pikemen had been entirely slaughtered. The king's standard moved from the mass of corpses and toward the city itself.

Grancaliga remained still as he watched his colonels issued frantic orders. The remaining soldiers in the room kept calm.

"Nervous?" Kara said.

"Hardly. I've been in this position many times."

"Then there's no reason for us not to continue with the ceremony, is there?"

"It is because I am so confident in my men that I postpone it. I won't let anyone say I needed to become a god to vanquish Telman."

"It's not just Telman you fight. How do you think he amassed such an army?"

Grancaliga withdrew and spoke privately with a courier. "Have the castle defenses put on alert."

"They already have, sir. The reserves are still in their barracks."

"Have them woken, but don't deploy them yet."

Returning to the window, he found the battle had now reached the city walls. He concealed his anger with a tight fist as the unsecured gates flung back and the enemy streamed into Merce Haelle. By the time more defenders had arrived to hold them back, numerous street blocks were overwhelmed.

"The city is lost," Grancaliga said. "Pull our men back to the castle."

A watchman on the battlement outside the window flashed a message flag to a bugler on the castle's lowest level, who then lifted his instrument and sounded general retreat. The defenders fending off attackers in the alleys and streets fell back in an organized manner toward the drawbridge and began filing inside. More and more enemy infantry swarmed through the three city gates, threatening to cut off Grancaliga's men still outside the castle.

"Perhaps Telman might let one survivor live," Kara said.

"I personally turned the tide of more desperate battles than this before you were born," Grancaliga said. "I know this castle well. While I was hunting for you, it was resupplied and armed. With my men, I could hold it for years…whether I be a god or not."

Kara ignored him as she watched the battle unfold through the window, her eyes never blinking. "I now know battle from your perspective, general. Soon, you will know mine."

The fighting moved closer to the castle. The drawbridge was overflowing with men desperate to enter before the order was given to close it. Grancaliga waited for as long as he dared, then signaled the bridge to raise. Soldiers pushed through into the castle courtyard, while the remaining troops left outside were swiftly overrun.

"Let us see how well prepared they came," Grancaliga said. "I see no catapults or engines in their midst."

Unable to cross the wide, deep moat, Telman's army began to toss garbage and refuse into the water. Their work slowed as archers on the battlements kept them pinned behind large wicker barrier. Gradually, makeshift crossings appeared in the moat at various points. Before they were complete, the enemy stormed across them and threw themselves against the high castle walls. Ladders, grappling hooks, and other climbing implements followed.

Soon the castle's front wall was lined with men scurrying up to the top. Many fell, but as they dropped, three more took their place. Eventually, some reached the top but were easily pushed back as additional heavy swordsmen reinforced the defenses.

The struggle went back and forth as Grancaliga paced the room, never taking his eyes off the castle walls. Kara was equally fixated, her hands clasped in prayer.

Eventually, the attackers withdrew across the moat and stood on the outskirts of the town while the castle defenders rejoiced.

"The first of many assaults," Grancaliga said. "Each shall be as easily repulsed."

Kara acted as though she hadn't heard him.

A rumble shook the floor, the chandeliers swinging widely above them. Then a section of the castle's front walls stirred before collapsing into a heap of stone. A thick, heavy cloud of dust swept over the battlements and into the air as the wind blew it upward. When it had settled, a large gap in the wall appeared before them.

"How could they have tunneled it so quickly?" Grancaliga said.

"It was always there," Kara said. "Telman knows this castle better than anyone; his family built it."

A thundering cry reverberated through Telman's ranks as his light infantry charged once more across the moat and into the breach. Disoriented still, Grancaliga's men struggled to regain their composure. A call from the bugler roused them. Retrieving their fallen weapons, they converged at the breach and struck hard against their foe.

"They'll never break through," Grancaliga said. "Once they withdraw, the wall will be repaired by morning. Telman used his best secret against us for nothing."

The two observed the fighting as Grancaliga's men formed a collective shield wall, preventing Telman's forces from exploiting the breach. The more they solidified their position, the more anxious Grancaliga grew.

"Get my colonels to the tower," he said to a courier. "We're holding the ceremony now."

Under escort again, Kara followed behind the general as they proceeded from the great hall toward the mountain summit.

"Are you that uncertain of victory?" she said.

"I'm not postponing my godhood any longer. That battle is over. Your divine pleas did nothing."

"Yet."

They reached the top of the tower, where all the preparations Kara had dictated were present. An altar covered in red cloth was placed along the side of the tower overlooking the lower castle and Merce Haelle. A large candlestick sat on it, a ceremonial sword beside it. Kara broke from her escort and placed the sacred texts and crown on the table. Surrounding the outer rim of the tower were guards uneasy in their impractical ceremonial garb.

The colonels appeared at doorway and bowed in front Grancaliga. "The line is holding, sir."

"When this affair is completed, I will personally take charge of the defenses."

Approaching the altar, Grancaliga knelt before Kara with his bent arms stretched out. "The time has come to fulfill your promise."

Nodding slowly, Kara lit the altar candle and picked up the manuscript. Turning to a marked page, she gave the sword a special blessing. When she was finished, it glowed a fiery red.

"Look!" a colonel said.

Everyone turned to their left, where on the castle wall just below the tower, a cloaked figure clung to the side. A watchman above stoked his fire until the light brightened the surface to reveal a person climbing the thick vine that covered the castle wall like a spider's web.

The watchman tried to shoot him, but the intruder sent an arrow straight into his eye. As the man fell off the wall, Grancaliga noted Arthema's distinct white bow in the man's hands.

"Jed," Kara said.

"Kill him," Grancaliga said.

The guards armed with crossbows lined the wall and fired in unison. The arrows struck near Jed's face and side, bouncing off the thick stone with a loud clack. Kara fell to her knees near Grancaliga, her hand covering her mouth.

"He will die," Grancaliga said. "You can either watch it, or not."

Her tears drying immediately, Kara rose to her feet and began reciting from the text. The ceremonial guard grew close as they listened to her mysterious chant. With her right hand extended out above him, her gentle voice turned deep and low.

Above them, darkened clouds formed and swirled as though caught in a vortex. Lightning raced across the sky like a wild stallion. Grancaliga remained still throughout the chant and the roar of thunder and the ongoing click of arrowheads against rock.

A man cried out, followed by urgent calls to pull back as watchman retreated to the center of the tower. Kara and Grancaliga were oblivious to it, as though caught in a same trance.

Kara then gripped the blade in her hand, placing the flat of the sword on Grancaliga's head. She recited a final verse that brought a pillar of fire from the clouds down on him. All his men gasped at first, only to feel no heat from the flames, while Grancaliga still knelt unharmed within. The bright inferno ran through him and pierced through his eyes and limbs. He leapt up and cried out as the blaze rose back into the sky and rolled into the clouds before vanishing.

On the far side of the tower, Jed climbed over the parapet. The guards formed around him to attack, until they heard Grancaliga stir.

The general got up from his knee. He looked no different than he had before. But all could sense a mystical new power within him that seemed to flow through them. Kara moved back to the altar as Grancaliga clenched his fist and laughed at Jed. His voice was now soft and gentle, but somehow terrifying.

"You're too late. It is over."

The guards pulled back, allowing Jed to approach. His face was concealed underneath his cloak hood. His bow was strapped to his back, his hands at his sides.

"What do you intend to fight me with?" Grancaliga said.

Jed was still. Then he brought a sword from inside his cloak and held it with a high guard. Its appearance provoked no response from the watchmen or the soldiers or the colonels until they saw the hopeful look on Kara's face.

"Ah, so it is real," Grancaliga said. "How funny is it that legend and myth is so often true."

Glancing at the crown, he gestured to Kara. "You've made me a god. Now make me king."

The young girl laughed. "You first mocked me for bringing it. I brought it, because I know you. You don't know yourself at all."

"Crown me, or pay the consequences."

"I'll pay it. The price for crowning you is higher."

Enraged, Grancaliga drew his great sword and lashed out at Kara. She fell before the altar, a ghastly wound in her side. Before anyone could speak, Grancaliga grabbed the crown and, despite baffled look on his men, placed it on his head. As soon as it came to rest, the crown became like a sun, radiating streaks of light that raced into the sky. When the light faded, Grancaliga turned to those before him and raised his hands upward

"All shall bow before me!"

As soon as he finished speaking, the battle below them ceased. Whether friend or foe, the combatants knelt in submission. The colonels and watchmen and soldiers on the tower did the same, so that all but one held their head low in servitude.

Grancaliga watched Jed remain upright, then scoffed. "I shouldn't be angry that you stand. After all, you're not Forenian."

Taking several steps forward, Jed stopped and threw back his hood. Before it fell, Grancaliga recoiled. The boy's face was now white as theirs, his light gray hair short and cropped. His eyes flared with the same amber hue.

His voice was now eerily similar. "You were saying?"

"What do you want?" Grancaliga said.

"Your head—crown on it or not."

"Once more, I should be more thankful than furious. Because of this foolish girl, I have both crown and texts in addition to godhood. To think I was once willing to accept mere guardianship. Now I am more than even a god; I am the god-king who shall rule eternal. With the girl dead, none shall know what the texts say, except what I say is written in them. And thanks to you, I will also have Impora as further proof of my divine claim. If ever my rule were to be questioned, these shall put to rest any argument to the contrary."

"Impora's in my hands, not yours."

"That will soon change."

"You still won't wield it."

"We'll see."

His hand raised to the heavens, Grancaliga cast a power spell so that the sky became an inferno; cradling flames in his hands, he channeled it at Jed, who easily extinguished them with Impora.

"That won't work," Jed said.

His great sword in hand, Grancaliga came up to the boy. "My gratitude is only greater. Now I will get to kill you with my own hand, not by divine powers."

"I'm still alive."

"Enjoy your time left, if you can."

With a great war cry, Grancaliga leapt at Jed and brought his sword down with all the might he could summon. The boy evaded the strike as it cut through stone like butter. He then swung at his side, almost wounding the self-appointed king. Grancaliga jumped back and then struck again, missing. He then threw spells to distract, but soon realized Impora's wielder was more than able to stop them, and even when he drew lightning from the sky, Impora fully absorbed it without harm to Jed.

The fight quickly turned into a frantic trade of strokes and parries. Those witnessing watched in awe as the two opponents pursued each other across the mountain's treacherous summit. Despite his enormous height, Grancaliga was unable to bring his full weight against Jed, who dodged every fatal strike and flipped away whenever he was about to be cornered.

Initially on the defensive, Jed then struck back against the god-king, a ferocity in him that left Grancaliga deflecting powerful strokes. With swing after swing, Jed knocked him off balance, his aggression intensifying with every successful strike.

"So you want to be king?" Grancaliga said. "My men will never follow you. You'll never be a Forenian. Impora will never change that."

"Your head is enough."

The fighting moved up toward the summit. Pushing up the slope, Jed hacked through rock as his sword came down hard against Grancaliga's. The force sent him reeling backwards. Enraged, he counterattacked, but Jed sidestepped and tore through his cape.

"You're alone," Grancaliga said. "Now all Forenia submits to me. Even Telman somewhere is on bent knee."

Using his frame like a battering ram, he tried to knock Jed off the slope. Jed jumped back to ward off a series of fast attacks.

The fight turned savage. Grancaliga was like a feral animal as he lunged at Jed, who in response pushed his full weight against the larger man. Whenever it appeared Grancaliga was about to make a fatal blow, Jed broke out of the trap and delivered a hit more painful to the general's pride than his flesh.

The duel grew even more ferocious, and gradually the two hacked away at the other's armor. Were it any other weapon, Grancaliga would have been impervious, but Impora's edge tore at his body. His men soon became nervous as they observed him hesitantly confront Jed after a brief respite. With his divine powers, he summoned a rainstorm from the clouds. Thick droplets fell like blood from his blade as he raised it high.

He rushed at Jed and as his opponent brought his sword down, thrust forward with a crooked strike. An instant later, Impora lay a distance from them by the parapets.

Grancaliga's sword went for Jed's neck, but the boy dove beneath the blade as it swung over him. Rolling across the ground, he snatched Impora and while still on his back held off another killing stroke.

With their backs facing, the two then turned and attacked simultaneously. Their blade clashed as their hilt guards locked together. They pressed against the other with all their strength. At first, Grancaliga brought himself down upon Jed so that the younger warrior was nearly brought to his knees. But just as his leg about gave way, his limbs stiffened. Pushing up and back, Jed gradually gained a footing and slowly stood fully upright. The energy harnessed with the two swords was so great it billowed into the sky. It was impossible to tell whether it was tears or raindrops trickling down their faces as they pressed close.

Grancaliga shouted above the storm raging over them. "You can't win."

"How so?"

"Did you not come for the girl?"

Jed looked over at Kara. Though still conscious, her face conveyed imminent death.

"Even if you defeat me, she dies," Grancaliga said. "Will my crown comfort you then?"

Jed pushed harder.

"This is why I always won," Grancaliga said. "I was willing to sacrifice everything and anything to achieve victory. She is the price for yours."

Giving him one last shove, Jed let go of his sword and ran over to Kara. Cradling her head by his side, he reached into his things. As her eyes closed, he poured a tiny drop from a bottle.

Nothing changed. Then her eyes opened. She touched at her side where Grancaliga had struck. Though the dress was still torn, she gasped in relief before noticing Jed's empty hands.

"Why?" she said. "You should have let me die."

The men assembled watched in disbelief, then stepped aside as Grancaliga approached with Impora now in his hand. Standing above them, he chuckled. "A noble, but futile gesture. You gave her only a few more seconds of life, at the cost of victory."

He then turned to Kara. "You said your place was wherever someone opposed me. It seems that place is right here. In a moment, no such place will exist or will ever exist again."

Bringing Impora high above his head, Grancaliga held his stance as his men waited for the final strike. He remained still as rain dripped down his clothes and robe. Her head bowed, Kara raised it when a long time passed and found Jed staring up at a state-like Grancaliga. He had the look of a man who knew the future but could not change it.

Impora then came down with both hands and pierced flesh and garment. A terrible groan broke through the storm's noise. Pools of blood formed at Jed and Kara's feet as small streams flowed off Grancaliga's boots.

Grancaliga dropped in front of them, his face bearing a strange distant expression. When his hands finally let go of Impora, the blade remained inside his chest, the tip plunging out his back. A blue aurora emanated from the sword as it seemed to drain Grancaliga of his divinity. When the aurora vanished, Grancaliga's eyes were as dark as his flesh.

The rainfall ceased immediately. Grancaliga's soldiers stared blankly at their dead commander's body. Throughout the castle and Merce Haelle, all got up from their bowed stance as a single people. The hostility between them earlier that night was gone.

Kara touched Grancaliga's body as she spoke to Jed. "Why did he kill himself?"

Jed retrieved Impora and held it by his side. "He didn't. Forena killed him."

"You knew he'd never be able to use it against you?"

"Yes."

She withdrew as the colonels approached Jed. Without a word, they snapped to attention and saluted him. Witnessing the gesture, the soldiers and tower guards did the same. Kara took the crown from Grancaliga's head and placed it on the altar.

"Why are you crying?" Jed said.

"Is it truly over?"

Jed went back to the body. Kara covered her eyes and turned as he struck the corpse. Blood fell from his grim face as he faced her.

"It's over," he said. "Crown on it or not."

***

Telman leaned against the parapet with Jed beside him as the dawn's rays appeared over the Perelor Mountains and brought light onto the distant plains where enemy corpses still lay. The royal banner now flew at the corner of every watchtower and at the castle gate.

Smoke still rose from all points of Merce Haelle, the streets gutted with wreckage from the night's battle. His men now patrolled past homes and shops where Grancaliga's forces had only hours before had stood in total command. The dead general's men had been disarmed, but freed. They worked along the roads clearing the rubble as common people stared down from their upper-story windows.

Telman appeared disheveled, his clothes tattered and caked in mud. However, he smiled broadly as he patted Jed on the back. "Even when all bowed to Grancaliga, I hadn't lost hope. I was a bit worried, though."

Jed nodded.

"The coronation ceremony is tonight," Telman said. "It seems they don't want to delay any further. Technically, the Elder Council is still the ruling body of the city and our kingdom. But I don't think they're going to be much trouble. I'm not sure what to do with them. Shall I show mercy, or execute them?"

"I wouldn't play God with Kara. I won't with you, either."

"I'm asking for counsel."

"Leave them in a cell alone with Grancaliga's head for a day or two, then let them go."

Telman chuckled, then became somber. "I suppose I can't talk you into staying?"

Gripping Impora in front of him, Jed shook his head.

"Perhaps Kara might persuade you?" Telman asked.

"She already tried last night. Twice."

"Well if that didn't work, then I expect nothing I say will."

"This is her world. I want to go to mine."

"Then between us, I'd still take you over a thousand Forenians. Grancaliga wasn't the cause of our problems. He tried to exploit our weaknesses, and almost succeeded. He didn't fail because we were stronger. There's still so much work left to be done, to rebuild, and now finally I assume responsibility. For so long, it's been outside of my control. Now, there's nothing to stop me but myself. And yet, for all the challenges that are ahead, I'm hopeful. Things were only going to get worse and worse until something changed. Now, we can start over."

The two left the battlements and walked to the center of the tower. Kara appeared wearing an ice-blue gown and white-hand gloves, the Varexians accompanying her. She put away a moist handkerchief in her hand and tried to avoid looking at Jed as she greeted Telman.

"All the preparations are ready," she said. "We'll hold the feast in the great hall once the ceremony is completed."

"Very good," Telman said, turning to the Varexians. "Have the scouts returned?"

"Yes, sir. They've reported news of our victory to the nearby towns. The troops there have complied without protest."

"I imagine Grancaliga's captured banners have helped."

"Or his sword and armor. There are none like them elsewhere."

"There is none like Impora either," Kara said.

"I'm glad I was here to help, but this isn't where I belong," Jed said. "It's time for me to go home."

Producing one of the manuscripts, Kara opened the book and pinched one of the pages with her gloved fingertips. "This is the Sojourner Prayer to wish someone a safe journey as they depart." As she recited it, she paused repeatedly until her wet handkerchief remained in her hand. When she was finished, she kissed Jed on the cheek. He briefly touched the length of her hair before pulling away.

"Simply pray it, and Impora will take you home," she said. "It's the one legend of ours I wish weren't true."

"A part of me wishes it, too."

Telman offered a hand of farewell. Jed accepted it, then embraced him tightly.

"If anyone deserves to find peace, it's you," Telman said.

"Long live the king."

Raising Impora once last time above his head, Jed gazed up at the sky and prayed. A breezeless whirlwind formed around him, sparks crackling as the area around him became opaque. He got one final look at Kara smiling hopefully at him before she vanished, and his feet left the ground. Swirling around the outer edges, he rose higher and higher, faster and faster, before his whole body shot out from the world, and the sword disappeared from his hands. In the void, he heard Forena whispering to him:

"Well done. Your wish is granted."

EPILOGUE

Jed found himself sitting on the park bench in front of the local baseball field. Before he bothered to look at himself, he glanced at the tree behind him and found nothing. He then examined his hands and face, wondering if it had all been a dream.

He heard his name called out in a formal tone. To his right, a tall, older-looking version of himself marched toward him wearing jeans and a U.S. Army T-shirt. Jed would have flung from his seat to greet his father, but instead, he got up slowly and walked up to him with a collected demeanor. When they reached each other, Jed smiled and shook his hand before hugging him.

"How have you been, son?" LTC. Hayes said.

"Well, sir."

The two were silent for a while.

"What is it, sir?" Jed said.

"You seem different…what have you been up while I was away?"

Jed's cheeks became red. "Nothing bad, sir."

"I know." He clapped his son on the shoulders. "You've changed. You have the kind of look my men had after they came back from their first mission. What's your mother had you doing?"

"Nothing. She's been fine."

"I'm not blaming anyone. I feel…I don't know…you're not as uncertain like you used to be. You're…you're talking to me like a man."

"Thank you, sir."

Pulling two gloves and a baseball from his sports bag, LTC. Hayes tossed the ball into the air. "How about we finally have that game of catch I promised you?"

He put his arm around Jed and led him to the empty baseball field. Out the corner of his eye, Jed looked to his left and saw the girl he had previously noticed reading the book. She was facing toward him, but too far away to know if she looked at her book or elsewhere.

He and LTC. Hayes played catch for a while. At one point, Jed threw the ball to his father, who caught it and then took his glove off to study Jed carefully.

"You can tell me anything, son," he said. "I have no suspicions."

"I can't explain it, but I know you'd be proud if you had been there."

His father nodded his head, slipping his hand back into the glove. "I believe you. When you wanted to join Junior ROTC, I was hesitant. I wanted to know it was something you were fit for. I think I know now. We'll get that taken care of soon."

"Thank you, sir!"

Winding his arm back, his father tossed the ball too high over Jed, who scrambled after it as it rolled on the ground and up the small hill to where the girl read. He took a closer notice of her. She seemed about his age with light blonde hair, wearing a light blue skirt and sitting barefoot with her shoes beside her.

He bent down to retrieve the ball and looked up to find her smiling at him.

"What are you reading?" he said.

She giggled. "Judging by the look on your face as you daydreamed over there, I'd say the same story."

Jed was still. His father patiently waited for him on the baseball field.

"I'm curious to know how the story ends," Jed said.

She looked up from her book, giving him a cryptic smile. "As good as that daydream went, I think…perhaps even better."

ABOUT THE AUTHOR

T.J. Martinell is an author, writer, and reporter frequently seen roaming the Cascade Mountains in the Pacific Northwest. He has written extensively about gun rights for the Tenth Amendment Center, a constitutional think tank. A variety of essays and short stories of his have been featured at *Terror House Magazine* and *Punch Riot Magazine*. Visit his personal site at *TJMartinell.com*.

terrorhousepress.com

Made in the USA
Monee, IL
02 December 2021

83737256R00062